Dalia,

Read and Enjoy!

Ruth Callick
2017

Run from a Shadow

Run from a Shadow

Ruth Callick

RUN FROM A SHADOW

iUniverse books may be ordered through booksellers or by contacting:

iUniverse
1663 Liberty Drive
Bloomington, IN 47403
www.iuniverse.com
1-800-Authors (1-800-288-4677)

Because of the dynamic nature of the Internet, any web addresses or
links contained in this book may have changed since publication and
may no longer be valid. The views expressed in this work are solely those
of the author and do not necessarily reflect the views of the publisher,
and the publisher hereby disclaims any responsibility for them.

Any people depicted in stock imagery provided by Thinkstock are
models, and such images are being used for illustrative purposes only.
Certain stock imagery © Thinkstock.

ISBN: 978-1-5320-0569-5 (sc)
ISBN: 978-1-5320-0568-8 (e)

Library of Congress Control Number: 2016913623

Print information available on the last page.

iUniverse rev. date: 09/23/2016

A heavy sigh escaped Casey Hammond as she waved after the jet that had just lifted off with her brother and his new wife aboard.

"Don't look so depressed," her cousin said with a grin. "That brother of yours hasn't left for Outer Mongolia, and you will be seeing him again."

"Not for a good six months. Oh, Donald, I'm going to miss Henry being around!"

Donald Hammond sent his cousin another grin. "That isn't what you said yesterday."

She giggled in spite of herself. "That's because he was so darn exasperating! I hope I'm not like that when I get married."

A rumble came out of Donald. "You'll probably be worse."

Casey punched him lightly in the arm. "Some cousin you are!"

"The best you've got…Are you sure you won't come to the coast with the rest of us? There's plenty of room, and it won't cost you a cent."

Casey shook her head. "Thanks anyway, Don. You go have fun. I've got plenty to do to keep me busy."

"You're sure?"

"Positive! Now go, before they decide to take off without you!"

Donald gave her a quick hug. "Okay. I'll see you in a few days."

Casey stood and watched her cousin disappear through the airport lobby. It would have been fun to fly over to the coast for the long weekend with Donald and his friends, it would have been a great way to spend part of the vacation she had left, but she didn't trust small planes, any plane actually. Besides, she would have been a third wheel and that would have made things too uncomfortable for everyone.

She glanced again at the sky where the jet had long since disappeared and silently wished her brother a happy honeymoon. They were heading up to Alaska where he had just been promoted. And they would be spending part of their honeymoon searching for a house. "Good luck," she whispered to them both.

A light touch on her arm brought her back to the present. "Excuse us…madam?"

Casey turned and looked down to find two young boys standing nervously by her side. The older couldn't be much older than ten, the younger, about six. Their clothes were crumpled yet clean; their hair slightly disheveled. They looked tired and troubled and more than a little apprehensive. Casey's heart went out to them.

"Is there some way I can help you?"

It was the older of the two that replied. "You can tell us where the bus…station will be?" His clear, polite voice held a definite accent. German, or maybe Scandinavian, she wondered? Both boys were fair, blonde, and blue-eyed.

"I'm sorry," she told them gently. "I'm afraid all the buses are on strike. None of them are working," she added seeing the look of incomprehension that passed over the older. "Can I get you a taxi?"

"A taxi?" It was apparent the boy had no idea of the word's meaning.

"A car," Casey said, "That will take you where you want to go…You aren't lost, are you?"

There was a definite shake of the older one's head as his arm tightened around that of his younger brother. "Father says we are to go to the bus station, to go to Brickett."

Casey gave a start of surprise. She had taken it for granted that the boys had wanted to go into the city. Brickett wasn't in the city. It was a small town some forty miles away.

Casey smiled ruefully at them. "You'll have to forgive me. I had the wrong bus system on strike."

"The bus will go to Brickett, then?"

Casey nodded.

Relief seemed to ease some of the apprehension. "You will tell us where to find the correct bus station?"

"It's mid-town." Her eyes glanced around them came back to the two boys. Misgivings were beginning to formulate at the back of Casey's mind. "The two of you are by yourselves?"

The older seemed to ignore the question. "Father said we are to find Uncle Dajon in Brickett. He is our family." His eyes flickered nervously around the airport's lobby.

"Where is your father?"

The boy seemed to tense as his eyes turned back to her. "He cannot...join us yet," he told her.

"You couldn't stay with your mother?"

His head shook. "Our mother is no longer alive."

Casey bent down to the two young boys. It was evident they were brothers, for they looked alike despite the fact that the older was taller and more solid; the younger smaller and slimmer. "So you are to stay with your uncle in Brickett until your father can join you?"

The older of the two nodded. "Please, madam. We must get to the bus station...to Uncle Dajon very quickly."

Her misgivings grew with the words *very quickly*. Casey again glanced around. Adults were going here and there but none seemed concerned about the two boys. She spotted an airport official.

The boy's eyes must have followed hers. "No!" he cried out in pure agony. "You must not take us to your authorities. *Please*! You must not! They will stop us from reaching Uncle Dajon and we *must* reach our Uncle Dajon!" he cried. "We must!"

Casey's heart caught at the pure panic of both boys. The younger had begun to cry and the older was ready to bolt. Already his eyes had gone frantically to the door leading outside. "Easy," she said soothingly pulling his attention back to her. Her voice was quiet. "Just tell me honestly, are you running away from your father?"

The boy's head shook adamantly. "It is Father who told us to go to Uncle Dajon...*Please*, madam. We *must* get to our Uncle Dajon. Please show us to the right bus station," he begged beseechingly, "Please."

The panic and pleading and tears tore at Casey. She knew by all rights she should turn them over to the authorities; let them handle the two children. But glancing at the agonizing fear in their young faces and the beseeching hope in their eyes, she just couldn't. It was obvious they had been through an ordeal; a rather tense, frightening ordeal by their looks. An ordeal that wouldn't be over with until they reached their uncle.

Casey knew suddenly, that right or wrong, nothing would stop her from helping them do just that. They didn't need the authorities to put them through any more fear or hassles or aggravation. They needed only to reach their uncle without further delay. She would see to it personally.

She stood and determinedly held out her hands to them. "Come. Let's get you to your uncle."

"You would take us to our Uncle Dajon?" There was both doubt and an agony of hope in his voice.

"Yes, I will take you to your Uncle Dajon," she said pushing away her lingering doubts and misgivings. After all, it was just a short forty miles to Brickett.

The younger brushed the tears from his eyes and slipped his hand into hers. Casey looked to the older. He seemed to hesitate a moment before doing the same. He gulped shakily. "Thank you, madam."

"My name is Casey," she said with a reassuring smile. "Casey Hammond."

"T'Casey Hammond," the older said aloud, but to himself as if putting the name to memory. He swallowed and looked up. "I am named Cortney."

"And your brother?"

"Chenin," he said after a slight hesitation.

Cortney and Chenin. Unusual names, she thought, but somehow they seemed to fit these two young children.

Cortney was quiet after giving her their names and did not speak again until they reached the car park. Still, Casey couldn't help notice the apprehensive glances he cast behind him.

Disquiet ran through her. Who, or what, were they running from?

"Is this a taxi?" Cortney asked when she stopped beside the shiny blue Ford and unlocked its doors.

Casey smiled. "No. Not a taxi. Just a car."

"Your car?" He seemed surprised that she would own a car.

"My cousin's actually. My car is at the shop being fixed." She held the door open and the two boys climbed quietly into the front seat beside her, the littlest in the middle, the older by the window…to keep watch? Casey found herself looking back apprehensively at the entrance they had just left before turning back to Cortney. "Do you have your uncle's address?"

Cortney reached into his shirt and slowly pulled out a wrinkled envelope. "Here is the letter to Uncle Dajon from my father. His name and where he is to live is written on the outside."

Something inside Casey eased as she took the letter from him for it gave a certain amount of credence to the boy's story. It wasn't likely he would have a letter to his uncle from his father if what he said wasn't the truth.

The envelope was sealed. It was addressed to a Dajon Jairon with a full address. No return address was given.

Casey pulled out the maps of the area her cousin kept in his car and searched through them. She knew he had one of Brickett somewhere.

Relief filled her as she found it. Even better, it was a new, 1969 map, something that surprised her for she knew her cousin wasn't usually good about updating anything. She opened it, searching for the address.

The boys watched her. "You can get us to Uncle Dajon?"

Casey sent both boys a brief smile. "Yes. I can get you to your Uncle Dajon." She handed both the map and the envelope back to Cortney before she started her cousin's car and pulled out into the traffic.

"Will it take long?"

Casey shook her head. "Not too long. About thirty minutes." She caught her breath as a car narrowly missed her changing lanes as she entered onto the freeway. She shook her head. It was late for rush hour traffic, but it was rush hour traffic nevertheless despite being only Thursday. After all, it was summer and the Salt Lake area was a vacation spot for many. She passed a slower moving car then moved back into the slower lane. Both boys were staring rather apprehensively out the windows. "You aren't from the United States, are you?" she asked to draw their attention.

"No," Cortney said quietly. He reached up and fingered the medallion he wore around his neck.

Casey hesitated to ask any more questions. The boy was uneasy enough and she didn't want to frighten him or his brother anymore that they already were. Yet, despite such concerns, her curiosity eventually got the best of her.

"Have you been in the States long?"

Cortney seemed to hesitate. "Two days."

"Your English is good," she told him, wondering where the boys were from. Chenin had not yet said a word and Casey wondered if maybe he could not speak English.

"Thank you," Cortney replied throwing a nervous glance out the back window. "Our father taught us."

So his younger brother could speak the English language. Casey glanced down at him to find him clinging to his brother, his eyes closed. He looked all out.

"Where are you from?" she finally asked Cortney after another moment.

The look he shot her appeared guarded. "We have come from your...Disneyland."

It wasn't the answer she had hoped for but considering the boy's uneasy apprehension, she accepted it for the moment.

"Did you enjoy Disneyland?"

Cortney appeared to contemplate her question. "I enjoyed it very much. It is truly a magic kingdom. Someday I will like to go there again."

Casey grinned. "So would I."

"You have been there, T'Hammond?"

"Yes, I have been there," she said. "And please, Cortney, call me Casey."

The boy was silent a moment. "In Disneyland, what is your...favorite place?"

"That's hard to say." Casey let her mind go back to the amusement park. It had been years since she had last been there. "Almost all the places," she said to the boy, "but

I suppose if I had to choose one, it would be the Jungle Cruise." She flashed him a smile. "What about you? What did you enjoy the most?"

"The pirates," he said promptly. "Chenin did not like it, but I would go on it again, and again."

Casey laughed softly. "That, I'm afraid, is one ride I haven't been on."

"You have not seen the pirates?" He sounded surprised.

"Not as yet. The ride wasn't there when I was last in Disneyland." It had only opened two years ago. It was an attraction she was looking forward to seeing the next time she was able to visit the park. "Tell me what it was like."

Cortney seemed to sit up straighter. "You ride on a boat and it takes you down into a cave where there are pirates everywhere, some even shooting cannons at you from their pirate ship. They are singing and doing all kinds of funny things."

"Sounds fun," Casey said curving off the freeway onto the smaller highway. "Did your father like it?"

It was the wrong question to ask. Cortney's face closed and the apprehensive, guarded look was back. He again fingered the medallion as he stared out the side window.

Casey wanted to kick herself. She turned her concentration back to her driving. Brickett eventually came in sight and Casey pulled off the highway onto a side street bringing the car to a stop.

"Let me see the map and your uncle's address again," she said to Cortney.

His eyes met hers as he handed them to her. "I am sorry, T'Casey. You have been kind, and I have been... rude. Forgive me, I ask. I am sorry. It is just that..."

"It's all right," Casey said soothingly. "I understand. You have things on your mind." She touched his face lightly. "I won't pry, Cortney. I just want you to know you can trust me. I'll help you in any way I can. I guess right now that means finding where your uncle lives."

She checked the address on the envelope then studied the map as she looked for the easiest way to their uncle's street. It looked surprisingly simple.

Casey smiled as she handed both the map and the envelope back to Cortney. "We should be there in just a few minutes."

A sigh of relief seemed to escape him.

To their luck, the children's uncle lived on the Southwest side of the small town, not far from the main highway they had just exited. Casey had no problems finding the quiet street. The house itself was on the left and she easily made a U-turn and parked in front of it.

All three of them stared at it. The house had a cozy traditional cottage exterior. It was painted a light green with white trim. Two trees decorated the small yard that was surrounded by a white picket fence.

"This is where Uncle Dajon lives?"

"This is where he lives." Casey checked the address again, just to be certain then climbed out of the car. Worry was beginning to spread through her for the house looked dark and there was no car in the driveway. Not that that meant anything she assured herself.

Cortney swallowed and looked back to her. "You will come to the door with us, T'Casey?"

"I'll come." She ushered the two boys out of the car and onto the sidewalk. They walked through the picket gate and up the walk to the quiet house noting absently it had recently been painted. Casey, with a deep breath, knocked on the door. Silence met them.

She waited another moment then rang the doorbell. Again there was no response.

"He is not here?" A touch of panic was entering Cortney's young voice.

"He just may be out for a while," she said soothingly, glancing at her watch. After all, it was only 8:15. "Maybe he needed to run to the store." She rang the doorbell one more time. Though they waited, the house remained silent. No one appeared home.

Casey watched as Cortney swallowed hard and his hand tightened around that of his younger brother. The fact that his uncle was not home had apparently come as a shock to him; an unpleasant shock. He was likely scared and tired and probably hungry, and now he most likely didn't know what to do. He swallowed again.

"T'Casey?"

Casey smiled determinedly, taking their hands. "Come. I think we could all use something to eat then we can decide what to do while we wait for your uncle to come home."

The boys did not argue. Casey ushered them back into the car and took them to a small supper house she found near the highway. They settled inside. The boys were each given a menu, but neither opened it.

"We cannot read your English," Cortney said quietly when she looked questioning at him. "I would not know how to…order."

11

Casey removed the useless menus from them with an understanding smile. "I'll order for you, Cortney. What would you like to eat?"

"I would like a meat sandwich, if I may?" His eyes moved slowly around the room.

"And you, Chenin?"

Cortney's eyes came immediately back to Casey. "Chenin will want the same," he said quickly. Too quickly?

Casey eyed him with surprise as well as a touch of unease. It was almost as if Cortney did not want his younger brother to talk at all.

"A meat sandwich," she said, forcing her attention back to the menus. She ordered then settled back, watching the boys as their eyes roamed around the walls of the supper house, Cortney's always returning to the door. He was nervous again she noted as he fingered his medallion. It wasn't a big medallion. It was about the size of a silver dollar, and like the silver dollar, appeared to be made of silver. It was beautifully etched with a multitude of swirls.

"Would you like to learn how to read English, Cortney?" she asked in an attempt to distract him.

"I must," the boy said letting go of the medallion and bringing his attention back to Casey, "For I will live in America." He stopped and looked up questioningly. "T'Casey, why is it you speak English, not American, in these United States? Is this not America?"

"I suppose it's because our country once belonged to England, Cortney. English became the established language, although we have Americanized it."

"Americanized it?"

"We made it into our own language. Our English is different from the English they speak in England."

"I understand." But whether Cortney did or not, Casey could not be sure, for his attention had already slipped from language back to food. He was watching the waitress carrying a platter of food their way. She passed their table and delivered the platter to several couples sitting just beyond them. Cortney's face seemed to crumble in disappointment.

"Ours will be here any minute now," Casey said lightly.

He nodded and sat back but his eyes still followed the waitresses. "This is ours?" A waitress was heading directly toward their table.

It was, and Casey watched the two young boys down their food like two hungry wolves. How long had it been since they had last had a decent meal she wondered as she told them for the second time to slow down. Eventually they did, but it was only after they had cleared their plates of not only dinner, but of dessert as well.

"Are you full enough?"

They both nodded, Chenin already half-asleep now that his hunger was appeased.

"Good." Casey ushered the boys to their feet.

Cortney hesitated. "Are we going back to see if Uncle Dajon is home now?"

"Just as soon as I pay the bill," she said with a reassuring smile.

Chapter TWO

Dajon Jairon's home when they returned to it looked just as dark and empty as it had earlier. As before, there was no car in the drive. She knew it was useless to try knocking again but she walked the boys up to the door and knocked anyway, for their sakes. As she suspected, there was no answer.

Cortney's eyes filled with tears. "T'Casey. What do we do?"

"Hey, don't worry," she said soothingly. "I'll take you home tonight and we'll come back in the morning."

"You will take us home? To...your home?"

"If you have no objections. Your uncle most likely won't be back until late and it looks as if you could both use a good night's sleep...You'll be safer, Cortney," she said softly.

His eyes flew to hers and for a moment he was silent. "You will bring us back here again in the morning?"

She sent him a reassuring smile. "I promise, Cortney. We will come back again in the morning."

Casey couldn't tell whether that satisfied the boy or not. He looked unhappy as he followed her back to the car...and still nervous and scared.

Scared about what? That his uncle still wouldn't be there when they returned in the morning? That he would be? Or was it more than that? She shook her head. It didn't matter.

She would take them home. Let them have a good night's sleep. Tomorrow she would take them back to Brickett and put them into their uncle's care. She wouldn't think beyond that.

She turned back to her driving. The highway merged into the larger freeway as it neared Salt Lake City. Her apartment was tucked in Saltine, a small suburb on the other side of the city. It took another thirty minutes to reach it.

She pulled into its parking lot and parked then glanced again at the two boys. Her heart expanded. Both were sound asleep. Yet even in sleep they were clinging to each other, almost protectively, she thought. She found herself wondering again what the boys were frightened of...or who? Or was it simply fear itself?

She didn't know. She knew only that she wanted desperately to help them; to ease some of the worry and tenseness from them...to protect them from whatever shadows they were running from.

She climbed from the car. She managed to wake Cortney and helped him stumble up the stairs to her apartment, setting him in her front room chair while she went and retrieved Chenin.

She then fixed the pull-out bed of the sofa and helped both boys into it, clothes and all. Leaving them sleep, she went on to her own room and crawled into bed with a sigh. The children were safe for the night. Tomorrow they would be with their uncle.

Casey rolled over and slept.

She had barely woke come morning when her bedroom door opened.

"T'Casey?"

She opened her eyes. Cortney was standing beside her bed clutching a breakfast tray in his hands. Chenin was beside him.

"We have brought you breakfast."

Casey sat up and he placed the tray on her lap. It was laden with toast and scrambled eggs and a fresh cut banana. Chenin handed her a glass of milk to go with it. She stared at the breakfast, then at the two boys. "Cortney…"

"You have been very kind, T'Casey. We wanted to be kind in return."

"Thank you," Casey said, not knowing what else to say. She normally ate a much smaller breakfast but not for the world would she tell them so.

Cortney looked pleased as he stepped back. "You are very welcome." He turned to go, hesitated a moment, then turned back to her. "T'Casey?"

"What is it, Cortney?"

He came back toward the bed. "Are we still going to Brickett, to Uncle Dajon this morning?"

Casey smiled. "Yes, Cortney, I'm still taking you back to Brickett. We'll leave as soon as we've eaten. Okay?"

A relieved smile came out of him as he nodded. "Then we shall let you eat." He turned, ushering his younger brother out of the room, but stopped at the doorway. "T'Casey."

She looked up.

"Chenin," he said, "She is my sister, not my brother."

He left her and Casey sat back, again feeling caught in something beyond her. Chenin was his sister, yet she was dressed as he was, making it impossible to tell...making it impossible to be spotted by someone searching for a young boy and girl?

But who, and, why?

Casey once more pushed the questions away from her and began to eat. At the moment, it didn't matter who, or why. It mattered only that Chenin and Cortney wanted desperately to reach their uncle. And she was going to see to it that they did.

She eventually pushed the tray aside and dressed. The first thing she wanted to do was to get the children's uncle on the phone. She wanted to notify him of the children's arrival and help insure that he would be home.

The first thing, however, proved impossible. Dajon Jairon did not have a phone. Not even an unlisted one the phone operator told her through a certain amount of static. Casey said nothing to the two children. Instead, she ushered them both into her cousin's car.

Chenin again slid into the middle beside her. "We are to go to Uncle Dajon now?" Her voice was light and sweet, and definitely that of a young girl. It was no wonder Cortney had not allowed her to speak sooner. It would have been a dead give-a-way for anyone looking for a girl.

Casey grinned at her and nodded. "That we are."

The freeway was quite busy when they reached it, but it wasn't surprising. It was Friday morning rush-hour as well as the beginning of another summer weekend. Casey took her time.

They headed through the city and then out, passing the Great Salt Lake. The two children seemed to take more of an interest in their surroundings than they had the night before.

"That is a lake?" Chenin's voice was full of awe as she stared at the expanse of water.

Casey grinned. "That is a lake. It's about the largest lake in our country outside of the Great Lakes."

"The Great Lakes? You are saying you have lakes bigger than this one?" Even Cortney sounded impressed.

Casey nodded. "Quite a bit bigger."

The boy stared at the lake. "It is like the ocean," he said at last. "Thern is a small country. Our lakes are very small."

"Thern?" She had never heard of a country called Thern.

There was a moment of hesitation. "It is a little, small country between Sweden and the Soviet Union," Cortney said. "The Soviets, they now rule it."

Casey sent him a swift look. "The Soviets? Cortney, have you and Chenin *escaped?*"

The boy nodded. He stared out the window for several long moments, and then turned slowly back to her. "The Talent Corps, it was to go on tour. Chenin belongs. Because Father is an important...scientist, it was arranged that I could go also, to be with her. We went first to Berlin, also Vienna, to Paris, then to Disneyland here in your United States."

"Where your father arranged for you to escape." It made sense, finally; the fear, the nervous apprehension, the urgent need to reach their uncle.

"It was not terribly hard," Cortney said quietly. "Father gave to us Uncle Dajon's address and told us what we must do."

"And Seron helped," said Chenin.

"Seron?"

"He is one of the…instructors of the Talent Corps," Cortney said. "He took us secretly from Disneyland to the big airport and bought us tickets. He then…arranged it so that we would fly to your airport by ourselves."

Casey glanced at him curiously. "How did he get you safely away from the others and out of Disneyland?"

The boy's eyes met hers. "Seron took us to the bathroom when Chenin pretended to be sick. He quickly helped Chenin change into clothes like mine and he cut her hair to hide that she was a girl. We then rode the high, fast train to the exit and walked out. We took the small bus to the airport."

"Were you scared?"

"Yes," he whispered. He seemed to shudder and looked out the window. "T'Casey, how soon now?"

"Soon," she said catching sight of a sign for Brickett. "Just five more minutes." Her thoughts were flying. She had heard of adults from the Soviet countries defecting, but never small children, not alone as these two were. No wonder they had been so petrified.

Brickett came in sight and Casey took the same turn-off from the highway she had taken the night before. She had no problem once again finding the quiet street.

Chenin looked rather nervously at Casey when she pulled the car to a stop in front of a small white house. "T'Casey, this is not the same house."

"I know. Your uncle's house is across the street," Casey said, pointing to the house they had been at yesterday. The house looked less deserted in the morning light. And to her relief there was a car now parked in the driveway.

"Come on," she said lightly, ushering them out of the car. "Let's go meet your uncle."

The two children walked across the street with her, but both hesitated at the gate of the picket fence.

Cortney's eyes went to the house. "It is a big house."

"It is a beautiful house!" his sister said.

Casey glanced down at Cortney. "Nervous?"

The boy slowly nodded. "It is not easy to meet someone you do not know."

"I know," she said holding out her hand, "but you are a brave boy Cortney and he will be happy to have you."

Cortney took her hand and they walked through the gate and up the walk Casey praying that what she told the boy would be true. Climbing the two porch steps they reached the door.

Cortney gulped. "T'Casey? Shall I knock?"

Casey nodded and the boy knocked hesitantly on the newly painted door. They waited several minutes in silence.

"Knock again, Cortney," she said lightly. He did, louder this time, and almost immediately the door was opened by a middle-aged woman with hair just beginning to gray.

"Yes?" she asked politely, eyeing the three of them.

"We're looking for Mr. Jairon," Casey told her, her hands tightening around the smaller hands gripping hers.

"Jairon?" the woman said blankly.

Casey's heart skipped. "Mr. Dajon Jairon. We understood he lives here."

"Lives here?" The blank look suddenly gave way and she smiled. "Ah, Dajon Jairon. You must mean the couple that used to live here. I'm afraid they've moved. I bought the house from them just over a month ago."

Cortney's hand tightened painfully around Casey's and she gave it another reassuring squeeze. She looked hopefully at the woman. "Do you happen to have his forwarding address?"

"I'm afraid I don't," the woman said, dashing Casey's hope. She suddenly brightened. "But I'm sure Mr. Banning has it. They were very close friends, I believe."

"Mr. Banning?"

"In the white house across the street," she said, pointing across the road to where Casey had parked her car. "I'm sure he'll know how to get in touch with Mr. Jairon for you."

Casey thanked her and the three of them turned and walked back down the walk. Both children looked ready to cry.

"We'll find him," Casey said. "Don't you worry. Mr. Banning is sure to have your uncle's new address."

The boys said nothing but their grip tightened around her hands.

Casey led them across the street and up the front steps to the white house and took a deep breath. "You knock this time," she said to Chenin.

The girl obeyed without comment looking decidedly pleased when the door opened a moment later. A wirily old man with bright, twinkling eyes stood in the doorway.

"Mr. Banning?"

The man nodded. "At least that was my name when I woke up this morning." He winked at Chenin and Cortney. His eyes came questioning back to Casey.

Casey managed a smile. "We were told you might have the forwarding address of Dajon Jairon?"

His eyes again went to the two children, then back to Casey. "Ah, lass," he said on a sigh. "I'm afraid I don't. Dajon wasn't sure of it himself when he left and I forgot to ask for it when he called. But don't you worry," he added, seeing Cortney's hand tighten around Casey's. "His son should be by any time now. I'm sure he'll be glad to take you to his father." He smiled suddenly.

"Why don't the three of you have a seat," he said indicating the chairs on the front porch, "and I'll bring out some lemonade."

The man disappeared and Cortney looked questioning at Casey. She nodded and he let go of her hand and sat down on the patio glider. "You, too, Chenin," she said when the girl's hand tightened around hers.

"You will not just leave us?"

Casey squeezed her hand in assurance. "No, Chenin. I'm not going to just leave you. But we must wait here for your cousin. He'll be able to take you to your uncle. Now sit with Cortney."

The girl cast an uncertain look at Casey and slowly did as she was asked.

Casey sat down in one of the two chairs at the small, round outside table. She looked up as Mr. Banning came through the screen door balancing a tray. He set it on the table and smiled at Casey. "I hope you don't mind pouring? I'm afraid I've gotten shaky in my old age."

"Of course not," Casey said with a smile. She had liked the man instantly. She poured, handing a glass each to Chenin and Cortney and then one to Mr. Banning before taking one herself. His eyes were again on the two children. They had begun to move the glider with their feet. He glanced back at Casey, his voice soft.

"So they have escaped at last. Was it difficult?"

Casey shook her head. "Cortney says it wasn't, but they were terrified when I came across them." Her voice, too, was soft.

The older man nodded his head. "Their father?"

"I don't know," Casey said. "I believe he is still in Thern." She bit her lip. "Mr. Banning…"

"Karl, please."

She flashed him a half-smile. "Karl. Has their uncle Dajon…has he moved far?"

"A fair distance. They moved on up to the state of Washington."

Casey's heart sank. Washington. It was a large state and miles away. How could she hope to take them so far? She looked back at Karl.

"You must not worry," he said softly. "Keir will see to it that you get to his parents."

Chenin abruptly came over to the table. "Is Keir our uncle also?"

"He is your cousin," Cortney said following his sister. "He is the son of Uncle Dajon." The boy turned to Karl. "T'Banning, will our cousin be here very soon?"

"I can't really say, but he will be here today and, no doubt, be mighty surprised." He sent another smile to the three of them.

Cortney drew his attention again. "You have known my Uncle Dajon a long time?"

The older man nodded. "Yes, I have known him for a long time. Your cousin was just a wee lad when they first lived here. I miss them all dreadfully."

Casey looked up. "Mr. Jairon's son, does he still live in the area?"

Karl shook his head. "No. I'm afraid Keir, too, has moved to Washington."

"You said he would be coming to see you?"

"That I did. Dajon was unable to take his van when they moved. He left it here in my care until Keir could find the time to come pick it up and drive it home for him."

"Keir is driving to Washington then?"

Karl Banning nodded. "He is but there will be plenty of room for the three of you to go along."

"Two," Casey corrected softly.

"T'Casey!" Chenin cried. "You gave your promise to us you would not leave us."

"I haven't left you," Casey said gently. "But Keir is your cousin. I must turn you over to him when he comes. He'll see to it that you get to your uncle."

"You will not come with us, T'Casey?"

"I'm afraid not, Cortney. Washington is very far away. My home is here."

The boy looked away for a moment then back at Casey. "I will miss you."

"I know. But you will have your cousin."

Karl smiled at the two children. "You will like your cousin Keir. He is a fine lad, like his father. You will enjoy camping and fishing with him."

Cortney smiled tentatively. "I have never camped… What does it mean to camp?"

Karl smiled. "It's sleeping in the open, laddie, under the stars where you can listen to the trees whispering in the wind and hear the water trickling through the brooks. It's hiking through the meadows and eating freshly caught fish over an open campfire and seeing the sunrise sparkling in the morning dew."

Cortney's eyes shone. "Uncle Dajon, does he like to camp also?"

"That he does, whenever he possibly can. And it will please him and Keir both to have you to take fishing and camping and to do all kinds of other things with."

Casey smiled at the two talking as if they were old friends. It was a pity Karl Banning wasn't their uncle. He got along well with the boy. She glanced over at Chenin. The girl was kneeling on the porch stroking a fat tiger cat, singing to it softly in her native language.

Despite the short time she had known them Casey knew she would miss the two young children when it came time to leave them. Terribly. She sighed unconsciously then glanced up as a black car pulled to a stop across the street from her own. She held her breath, but let it out again when two men climbed out and started through the picket gate across the street. It was not Keir Jairon.

"*CORTNEY!*"

Chenin's voice was no longer singing, but filled with horror. "It is them!" she cried out to her brother. "It is Bruen!"

Cortney's eyes flew in the direction his sister was staring and the glass he was holding slipped from his hand. His face went white.

"Cortney?"

His terrified eyes looked beseechingly up at Casey. "It is them!" he whispered. "It is the nadarb. They will take us back!"

Casey's eyes again flew to the two men. No, three, she realized, for another was exiting the back of the black sedan and joining the others. They were just a few steps from the door, and it would open...

There wasn't a moment to lose. "Cortney," she ordered softly, "Get Chenin to the car."

The boy didn't waste a moment. He grabbed his sister's hand and ran silently, Casey no more than a step behind them. A startled Karl Banning stared after them.

Chapter THREE

Casey and the two children slipped into her cousin's Ford and the engine flew to life instantly. But it was almost too late. The kind lady who had pointed them to Karl Banning was now pointing to them. The three men began to move, much faster than Casey had expected.

Casey shifted into drive and Donald's car tore away from the curb and down the street. She held her breath as she swerved around the corner narrowly missing a taxi going in the opposite direction. Almost immediately she turned down another street heading toward the highway, hoping against hope…

Hope died as she spotted the black sedan in her rear view mirror. She had acted instinctively, but they, she suspected, had reacted with training. She turned another corner and then sped onto the highway.

"T'Casey!"

"It's all right, Chenin," she said, surprised at her own calmness, for her heart was thumping wildly. "They won't catch us." She glanced again in her rear view mirror. The black sedan was still a half a block behind them, caught behind several slow-moving cars.

Casey used the opportunity to put distance between them knowing full well that shortly the two lane highway would become four lanes then merge into six as it became freeway. She had no idea where she was going, only that she must somehow lose them. Instinct told her to stay near the city. It would give her a better opportunity to slip away so long as she avoided the city itself with its mammoth traffic jams.

The highway abruptly merged with the freeway and the two lanes became four. The black sedan shot around the slower cars and began to put on speed...more speed than Donald's old Ford was capable of.

Cortney sucked in a breath. "They are gaining!"

"I know, Cortney...Who are they?"

"They are the nadarb, the...the guards who were watching us and the talent corps. T'Casey!"

Casey's hands tightened around the wheel. She watched as the black sedan slowly gained. Her mind raced. The freeway itself, now three lanes in each direction divided by a cement barrier, made it harder to escape for there was no place to turn; no place to go except down an off-ramp, an action those in the black sedan could easily see. They would be right behind her.

Unless...

Unless she could use the spaced out off-ramps to her advantage! Her heart suddenly jumped as the idea took hold. Her mind spun. She would have to time it just right. And there would be no room for mistakes.

She concentrated on where she was, and what was ahead of her. Traffic, already busy, was increasing and would continue to increase the closer they came to the city. It was both an advantage and a disadvantage. She glanced back. The black sedan was still gaining despite the heavier traffic. Another fast moving vehicle slightly behind the sedan caught her attention, for it, too, was weaving quickly in and out of traffic. A highway patrol?

No. It was too long and too wide to be a highway patrol car. Besides, it was green and white…a Dodge.

She glanced up at the freeway signs and her foot eased slightly from the accelerator, decreasing her speed ever-so-slightly. If she could snake off on the Pepperride Exit she could take the old highway into Saltine.

"T'Casey! They are so close!"

There was panic in Cortney's voice. Casey smiled absently. "Why do you put the 'T' with my name? I noticed you used it with Mr. Banning's name as well."

The boy's attention was temporarily diverted. "It is a title of…respect. Like your Mr. or Madam."

"Do you use it within the family?" She glanced at the passing freeway sign, then back at the black sedan. It was coming up fast; almost too fast.

"Sometimes," Cortney said. He glanced out the back window. "T'Casey--!"

"I know," she said softly. The black sedan was directly behind them now, still gaining. It pulled into the left lane, intent on overtaking them. She pushed down on the accelerator again and her car spurted ahead. The black sedan's speed increased as well and it slowly began to pull up even with her cousin's car then began edging past it, most likely to pull in front of her and slow her down. It was what Casey had hoped for.

Without warning, she veered sharply to her right, across the slower lane, narrowly catching the freeway exit.

It wasn't the exit she had originally planned, but it would work out better overall. Or would it?

The green and white Dodge that had been gaining on both her and the black sedan came flying off the freeway behind her.

So there were two of them.

Casey hesitated only a moment before she crossed through the red light at the end of the off-ramp and raced up the freeway on-ramp on the other side. Unless the black sedan had virtually come to a stop, it was now ahead of her, and more than likely taking the next exit in order to find her again. Her only problem now was the green and white Dodge. It was still on her tail.

"Cortney, watch for the black car," she ordered the boy, moving into the middle lane. The green and white Dodge moved up behind her. Its lights began flashing on and off.

Casey increased her speed. She passed the next exit but there was no sign of the black sedan. Good. That left only the one car...and the Pepperride turn-off.

She glanced back. The green and white Dodge was still behind her, its lights still flashing on and off. It was taking no chances in overtaking her. She wouldn't get away with disappearing a second time. She would have to rely on speed...and luck.

The Pepperride exit came and Casey took it as fast as safety allowed, barely missing a red light at the end of the off-ramp.

The green and white Dodge was not so lucky. She could hear the blare of its horn as it squealed to a stop.

Casey gave a heavy sigh of relief as she turned onto the country road that would take her to the old highway. She had a head start and knew she had to make the best of it. The old highway, although it was not used as frequently now that the freeway had gone in, was sure to be busy with the slower-moving travelers that were getting an early start to the weekend. If she gained a mile or two on the green and white Dodge, it would be difficult for him to make it up.

But he was faster than she expected. Within minutes he was back within sight of her rear-view mirror racing towards her, his lights still flashing. And worse, she realized, there was little traffic to hold him up on the country road.

Casey stepped harder on the accelerator, hoping and praying the highway was closer than she remembered. Five miles? He would have them by then, and with the road as empty as it was...

A whistle caught Casey's attention and her heart jumped. She had forgotten the railroad. Her eyes flew to the train, then to the crossing ahead. Could she make it? She had to! The thought of what would happen if she couldn't didn't bear thinking. She pushed the accelerator to the floor.

The driver of the green and white Dodge had also seen the train, for he began to gain with a tremendous burst of speed.

But it wasn't enough. Casey raced through the railroad crossing just as the bars began to lower. For a horrible second she thought the green and white Dodge was going to break through them, but at the last moment his brakes squealed and the train roared past.

Casey wasted no time. With her foot still on the accelerator, she raced to the old highway and headed for Saltine.

Chapter FOUR

Cortney sat watching diligently out the windows. "You have lost them," he breathed after a while.

"I believe we have." Relief filled Casey as she glanced again in her rear view mirror. There was no sign of either car.

But it wasn't over. Casey glanced down at Chenin curled tightly beside her, then over at Cortney who was beginning to settle. They still had to get to their uncle.

"T'Casey?"

"Let me think, Cortney."

The thought of turning the children over to the authorities did not even enter her head. This was her mission. She would put the children somewhere safe while she tried to get in touch with Keir Jairon or at least gained the address of his father. And the safest place?

It would have to be her apartment. But first she needed to exchange Donald's car for her own. She took the Saltine turn-off and headed into town. With any luck her car would be ready to go.

Luck, however, was not hers. The car was up on the racks, looking in worse shape than when she had brought it in.

"It will be another few days at least," Vince told her. "The parts most likely won't be in until Monday."

Casey thanked the older man with a tired smile and turned back to the children. So that was that. They were stuck with Donald's car.

"T'Casey?"

"It's all right," she said. "What we need now is a phone book."

"A phone book?"

"To see if we can find Karl Banning's telephone number," she said absently. She turned back to her mechanic. "Do you have one, Vince?"

"In the office, Casey. Over by the file cabinet there are several of them."

Casey found the pile of phone books on the floor and thumbed quickly through them until she found the one for Brickett…but there was no listing for Karl Banning.

"Blast!" she muttered, closing the book. She picked up the phone and dialed information. Again, she had no luck. Karl Banning's number was unlisted, something the phone company's operator wouldn't give out despite the fact she told him it was an emergency. That meant only one thing. She would have to drive back to Brickett.

"Will you phone him now, T'Casey?" Both children had stood by quietly watching her.

Casey shook her head, not bothering to answer. She borrowed paper and pencil from Vince and wrote out her address. Taking another sheet, she wrote Donald's name and phone number.

"Cortney, I want you to listen to me," she said turning to the boy. "I'm going to phone for a taxi. It will take you back to my apartment. I want you and Chenin to stay there and lock yourselves in. Don't open the door to anyone. Don't answer the phone. Just stay put."

The boy sent her a look of alarm. "But where will you be, T'Casey?"

"I've got to drive back to Brickett to see Mr. Banning, and to find your cousin."

"But, cannot—?"

"No, Cortney. If by chance I run into those men again, I don't want you with me." She handed him the paper with Donald's name and number. "Cortney, this is my cousin's phone number. If I don't come back tonight, I want you to call him. And keep calling him until he answers. His name is Donald. He may not be back for a few days, but he will be back. He'll help us. Just tell him everything and he'll see to it that you get to your uncle."

"T'Casey, no!" Chenin cried. "We will not go without you! You cannot leave us!"

"I've got to Chenin." She knelt down to the child. "I've got to find your cousin. It may take me longer than I expect, but you'll be okay. I promise. Now be a good girl and mind Cortney."

Casey phoned for the taxi, but was loathe leaving the two children when it arrived. Suppose they were seen, or couldn't find the key she had hidden, or ran into some other kind of difficulty?

She gave the driver the address of her apartment building and then slipped into the back with the two children. She knew it would be cheaper to just cancel the taxi and take them herself in her cousin's car, but she was too afraid the car would be spotted and with Chenin and

Cortney inside, it was too big of a chance. It was simply safer with the taxi.

Once they reached her apartment, she settled the children and made sure Cortney knew how to use the phone as well as the television. At the last minute she changed clothes and drew her free-flowing brown hair up into a ponytail in hopes of being less recognizable. Would it work? She stared at her five-foot-three frame in the mirror. Nervous brown eyes stared back at her. She could see no real difference except for the surface changes she had made. It would have to do.

Taking a deep breath, she checked on the children one last time, and with their promise to stay put and not open the door to anyone, she took the taxi back to the auto repair shop.

Nerves assaulted her as the taxi pulled to the curb and stopped just behind her cousin's Ford. Had her cousin's car been spotted during her absence? Were they watching her right now to see where she would go? Or, were they waiting for her? The fact that she had changed clothes and had pulled her hair back into a ponytail and was unlikely to be instantly recognized didn't help. She would have to walk over to Donald's blue Ford and then they would know.

For a brief moment, the thought of taking the taxi on to Brickett entered her head but she just couldn't afford it. No, it would have to be Donald's car.

Casey paid for the taxi then glanced around apprehensively as she walked to her cousin's car, but there was no sign of the black sedan or the green and white Dodge. With her heart pounding in quick rhythm, she climbed into it. She took time to hide her wallet under the seat before starting the engine. It would be disastrous if it was found on her, for it held her address and would lead them directly to Chenin and Cortney.

With her heart still pounding she pulled out into the traffic, her eyes everywhere. The freeway when she reached it was still busy and for the first half hour Casey did nothing but concentrate on the traffic always aware of the cars around her. She let out a relieved breath as she turned on the highway. There was still no sign of the black sedan or the green and white Dodge.

Her thoughts jumped ahead. Karl Banning was a smart man. He knew that Chenin and Cortney needed to get to their uncle. He would be sure to obtain their uncle's address this time. Or more likely, detain the children's cousin in hopes that they would be back.

With another glance in the rear-view mirror, she turned off the highway onto the road leading into Brickett. Her car slowed considerably. Suppose, just suppose, they were at Banning's waiting for her?

"No!" she cried aloud reprimanding herself firmly. Her luck couldn't be that bad. Besides, they had no reason to doubt that she and the children hadn't already obtained their uncle's address. As far as they were concerned, she was already speeding them on their way.

She turned the corner onto the street, then swerved precariously as a black blur whizzed past narrowly missing her; a black blur that looked very much like the black sedan.

Instinctively, Casey slammed her foot down on the accelerator and the Ford shot forward and past the Banning house. One glance in her rear view mirror told her she had been right. The black sedan had swung around, its brakes squealing in protest, and was now bearing down on her. They had recognized her as quickly as she had recognized them.

Casey groaned aloud as she once again maneuvered her way back onto the highway. She was only a car or two ahead of them. Heaven help her. How was she going to get away from them this time?

All too soon the highway merged into the freeway, turning from two lanes into four. The black sedan moved quickly up behind her, but despite its greater speed, made no move to overtake her. No. It would not make the same mistake twice.

Casey slowed to a more normal speed as the freeway widened to six lanes. She racked her brain for a way out; a way to escape the three men now chasing her. She wondered vaguely why they hadn't just called the authorities on her. Surely they had reported the children as missing by now. But they didn't act as if they had. If fact, they were acting as if this was some kind of undercover operation they wanted no one to know about – including the authorities.

Because they were foreign nationals? Not hardly.

It was more likely they would be drawn and quartered if their own government discovered they had lost the children she half-giggled.

She pulled herself up short. This was no laughing matter. Those foreign men were determined to get their hands on Chenin and Cortney; just as determined as she was to prevent them. And though they seemed reluctant to involve the U.S. authorities, she well knew all would be lost for both her and the children if the authorities did get involved. No. She was on her own here. She would have to wait, and hope and pray that somehow, something would come up and she would be able to break away.

And then what?

Then she would high-tail it back to her apartment and sit tight until Donald came back in town. It's what she should have done to begin with. They didn't know Donald. He would have no trouble being seen visiting with Karl Banning. They would have no reason to believe he was seeking the Jairon address.

She glanced again in her rear-view mirror. The black sedan was still back there keeping pace with her. She looked further behind the car wondering about the green and white Dodge. There was no sign of it, or was there? For just inside her vision there was a vehicle moving up, but it could be anybody as busy as the freeway was. Why invent more trouble, she scolded herself. She had enough trouble as it was.

Big trouble. To her dismay, she found herself caught suddenly in slowing traffic. She had come far too close to the city without realizing it and now she was caught in its bumper-to-bumper traffic.

The cars slowed to a crawl, then a standstill. Casey's eyes flew to the black sedan. For several minutes the men inside did nothing as the cars inched forward, stopped, inched forward again, stopped again. But then suddenly the door of the black sedan opened and a large man climbed out; the man Chenin and Cortney had called Bruen.

Casey sat watching him, too petrified to move. Only too late did she realize her car doors were not locked. She reached over in a panic but already the door was opened and the man slid into the seat beside her.

"You will do as I say," he stated, showing her the gun he held in his hand. His voice was deep and thick with accent…and deadly.

Casey shuddered.

"You will take us now to where you have left the Jairon children."

For several long moments Casey's mind ceased to function. Then, slowly as the traffic crawled on, she began to inch her car forward, edging it over to the right and off the existing freeway onto another. She had no idea where she was going. Her mind still refused to think. She was driving instinctively back out of the city, the black sedan never far behind. She did not even look for the green and white Dodge.

Slowly, she began to force her mind to function again as she drove. What was she going to do? Where was she going? She didn't know. She knew only that she would not lead them to the children. Her eyes flickered to the gun and again she shuddered. There was little doubt Bruen would use it if he was pushed.

Oh, Lord, she cried silently. How could she possibly keep them from Chenin and Cortney without getting hurt herself? She glanced around. She had merged onto the smaller freeway leading west, along the lake. But there was no place to go. No place. At least the traffic was flowing on the smaller freeway she thought innately.

"We will not wait long," the man beside her said, cutting into her thoughts. "You will take us to the children."

Casey again shuddered. What was she going to do? What?

Her eyes suddenly caught sight of the new Heinshire Mall. Could she? Chenin and Cortney's small, terrified faces crossed her mind and she knew she would try anything that might mean their freedom, and possibly hers. She veered off the smaller freeway and made her way down the street and into the mall's large parking lot bringing the car to a stop in one of the out-lying parking spaces. The black sedan stopped in the space beside her.

The gun beside her clicked. "The Jairon children, where are they?"

Casey shook, finding it impossible to find her voice.

"Maybe you would talk better with a bullet in your belly?"

She went white. She forced herself to answer though her shaky voice was no more than a whisper. "They're here. I...I left them here...at the movie theater," she added with a pure stroke of bravo.

Heinshire Mall, one of the newest and largest malls in the state had four movie theaters on the ground floor. The man stared up at the building a moment or two then said something in a foreign tongue to the two men from the black sedan. The door beside her opened and she was pulled from her cousin's car by a hefty man in a dark red shirt. If he, too, held a gun, Casey didn't see it though she didn't doubt it was there. Bruen climbed out from the other side.

"You will take us to them. Now!"

It was an order Casey had no chance of refusing. Bruen grabbed her arm, and after a short command to the third man, began walking her toward the mall entrance. The red-shirted man fell in step on her other side.

Casey shuddered again. She was taking an awful chance; a deadly chance. Although the guns were now out of sight, they were there and she knew neither man would hesitate to use them. If this didn't work…

The hand around her arm tightened and she led them slowly inside and down to the theaters, giving a silent prayer of thanks to find that two of the four theaters were showing G-rated films; one a Disney classic. It meant that being summer, the place would likely be packed with children of all sizes and ages. How would anyone be expected to remember one small boy and his sister even if they had seen them?

"They should be in there." Casey managed to point to the theater showing the Disney film. The two men exchanged glances. The rules were posted and clear. They had a choice, either they could send her in for them, or one of them could go in search, as it was theater policy that only one adult was allowed in to find a child.

It did not surprise Casey when the man with the red shirt disappeared into the theater, leaving her outside in the mall with Bruen. It did surprise her, however, when the doors opened a moment later and a troop of excited children came storming out, pushing past them.

The movie was over. Casey pulled her arm away from her startled captor and ran, darting into the nearest department store. She weaved her way around counters, found the stairs and ran up them to the second floor and back out into the mall.

What now?

Chapter FIVE

Casey's eyes darted in every direction. There was no sign of the foreign thugs, but she knew that wouldn't last. She had to move, had to find some way out of the mall and back to Donald's car without being seen. Was it possible?

It had to be!

She hurried down the mall's walkway, but darted back inside the nearest store as she caught sight of a familiar dark red shirt moving quickly. It was Bruen's companion; the one who had gone into the theater to look for the children. He must have come up the mall escalator. She watched him apprehensively from behind a book counter, hoping against hope that he would disappear.

He didn't, not at first. He stood looking around, his eyes everywhere. He must have thought he had spotted her for he suddenly darted into a store.

Casey took the opportunity and ran. It would be unsafe to go down the mall stairs. It was too open. Yet, she had to get downstairs and outside. She stopped momentarily behind a large planter, glancing around. What to do? Her eyes suddenly focused on the entrance of the high-class department store across from her; Macy's.

And Macy's had an elevator!

Casey with a careful glance down the walkway, dashed across and into the department store. She quickly wound around the counters looking for the elevator. To her relief the elevator was empty when she found it. She slipped in and closed the door, willing it to move. It seemed to take an age before it connected and made its downward decent. Casey bolted from it the moment the doors opened heading for the outside entrance. She cast an apprehensive eye around her as she ran but could see no one, not until she was outside.

There, standing only yards from Donald's car was the third man. He stood searching the outside grounds, a pair of binoculars glued to his eyes. Casey darted back inside Macy's, her heart thumping. Had he seen her? She doubted it as she watched him out the glass window. He was still searching with the binoculars.

What was she going to do? How was she going to make it back to the children if she couldn't get to Donald's car?

The bus line!

No. She dismissed the thought immediately. The city bus lines were still on strike. But the taxi service wasn't! If she could make it to the mall's taxi service drive she might have a chance.

But she was in Macy's and the service drive was outside of the Boyde Trentworth store, clear on the other side of the mall. She would have to go back down the center of the mall to get there. Or would she?

Casey glanced again outside the window. The third man still had the binoculars glued to his eyes, yet he was searching the parking lot, not the outside of the building.

She took a moment to reach up and remove the rubber band from her ponytail letting her hair cascade back down to her shoulders. She then eased through the door and back outside, glancing again at the man. His eyes were still trained elsewhere. With her heart in her throat, she took her chance and walked quickly down the sidewalk, afraid that if she ran it would draw his unwanted attention to her. She rounded the corner of the mall's building and out of sight of the man watching for her. Her speed increased.

Though she was fairly certain that the two other men would still be combing both floors inside the mall for her, she was taking no chances. Her eyes went everywhere, watching the doors for any sign of the man in the red shirt, or the other, more dangerous man: Bruen. The third man, she didn't worry about. She was out of his sight and she knew instinctively that he would remain by the cars to insure that she was not able to get back to Donald's and disappear.

She continued down the side of the building then around the next corner of the building as she headed toward the outside of Boyde Trentworth and the taxi drive.

Her heart jumped as she caught sight of it. After another quick glance around, she began running down the sidewalk toward it. There was a single taxi in the service area; two ladies just reaching it. Casey did not let that stop her. She pushed her way forward.

"Excuse me," she said, stopping the first of the two ladies from climbing into the lone taxi. "Would you mind terribly if I shared the taxi with you? Please. It's an emergency."

The two ladies looked up at Casey in surprise, not missing, she was sure, the desperation on her face. They looked at each other and then back at her. "Well, if it's really an emergency..?"

"It definitely is," Casey said, forcing a smile.

The ladies moved aside. "Oh course, then. We can call for another one."

Casey went weak with relief, but before she could move, a hand locked around her arm in a grip that hurt as a large man stepped up beside her; a man with a heavily accented voice. Bruen.

"Thank you, madam, but that will not be necessary. I am able to come and get my wife after all." Casey felt the hidden gun dig into her side.

The ladies eyed Bruen a moment before they hurried into the waiting taxi. Casey collapsed, but the sheer strength of the man held her on her feet. "Walk!" Bruen hissed.

Casey was too scared to do anything but obey. She could feel his anger and determination. She walked shakily beside him up to the far corner of the mall, then out into the parking lot. She made one attempt to break free and run but Bruen's grip tightened painfully preventing her from even moving from his side as he forced her to the waiting black sedan. There, she was shoved brutally into the back seat. She stared in horror as Bruen climbed in beside her.

"You are foolish," he stated thickly. "Now you will pay." His hand came hard across her face, sending her head spinning.

"The children, where are they?"

Casey opened her mouth but no sound came out. She knew with dead certainty that this was the end. She would not be coming out of this alive whether she turned Chenin and Cortney over to them or not.

The man's hand took hold of her chin and he forced her to look up at him. "I will ask once more only. Where are the Jairon children?"

Casey swallowed hard. His hand on her chin hurt; tightened painfully. "They're on their way to their uncle's," she cried out in agony. "On the bus!"

The hand tightened a degree more. "What bus?"

"The bus to Williamsport," Casey cried again with the first name that came to mind. "I put them on the bus to Williamsport!" Her eyes filled with tears.

He let her go but he wasn't done with her. "Where is Williamsport?" he demanded.

"I don't know," she wailed, "In Washington somewhere. I don't know!"

Bruen was silent a moment, his eyes watching her intently. "The address. I want it!"

Casey said nothing and his hand came hard across her face a second time. She saw red then…and heard echoes of swearing voices… of questions being asked…of flesh hitting flesh.

And then…nothing.

She was on a bed when she came to, in a cheap, dark motel room. Her head hurt abominably and she groaned soundlessly, unable to move. There was a gag in her mouth and her hands and feet were bound tightly behind her.

Tears stung Casey's eyes as she looked around the stark room. The heavy drapes were drawn, keeping the room dark, keeping her from any knowledge of where she was. The only light in the room came from a partially open door leading into the motel room beside hers. She could hear voices coming from the other side; heavily accented voices.

She groaned again. How long had she been here? Had they found her wallet? Were Chenin and Cortney still safe? Had Bruen discovered she had lied yet again?

The tears stinging her eyes began to slowly cascade down her cheeks as she thought of what lay in store for her...as she thought of Chenin and Cortney...and of Donald and Henry and home. Desperation filled her. She struggled unsuccessfully to untie the bonds holding her but she succeeded only in drawing them tighter. Exhausted, she gave up and silently cried herself back to sleep.

Movement woke her a short while later. Her feet were no longer bound and someone was untying her hands. Her head still pounded terribly and she groaned in protest.

"Good," a soft, male voice whispered. "You've come to." The gag was removed from her mouth.

Casey groaned again as she struggled to gain her equilibrium.

A hand immediately reached down and lightly covered her mouth. "Hush. You need to stay quiet." She was pulled her to her feet.

She swayed as her head reeled. His two strong arms caught her and she was picked up and carried quietly out into the cool air.

The man carrying her carefully eased the door closed behind them and started across the narrow parking lot. It was only then that Casey began to react. She was being moved by one of the men. He was younger than the two who had been with Bruen earlier, yet was just as strong and determined.

She began to struggle. She had to get away. Now, before Bruen and the rest joined him...before they could take her to places unknown! She had to!

But her head reeled and she couldn't even get her arms loose as the man's grip tightened.

"Easy," he murmured softly, close to her ear. He was hurrying toward several parked vehicles. Casey struggled even harder.

The man's grip loosened and he dropped her to her feet. "Casey, don't fight me," he ordered tensely with a slight shake. "We need to get you out of here before Bruen returns!"

Casey's stomach churned at the mention of Bruen. The man holding her pulled her quickly over to the nearby van and opened its passenger door. "Get in."

Casey hesitated, trying to assess what was happening. Was she being moved...or rescued?

"Please, Casey. We need to get out of here!"

But at that moment the sound of low, deep voices could be heard bringing the man's head up. Casey, still not sure what was happening, tried to bolt but she barely moved an inch as she was gripped hard and pushed against the van's side. Her head reeled once again and she cried out. Her cry was instantly cut off as the man's lips came down on hers in one long, silencing kiss.

Casey struggled a moment, then froze as she heard Bruen's angry voice intermingled with the other voices. Pure panic surged through her then. She tried desperately to pull away and run, but the man did not let her go. Neither did his lips leave hers. Not immediately.

She had to gulp for air when they did. "Inside!" was hissed as he thrust her up and past the front seat and into the back of the van. "I've got to get us out of here before he finds you're missing!" He was already behind the wheel. "Be still and stay down!" The engine came quietly to life, and without wasting a second, the van slipped noiselessly out of the parking lot and down the street before it picked up speed.

Casey wiped away the kiss that seemed to linger and sat on the floor of the van, her heart pounding in confusion and fear. She was unaware of her tears. For the first several minutes, the man at the wheel drove as if the devil himself was after him. Not that she minded. He was taking her from Bruen and his foreign cohorts.

For a moment that's all she concentrated on. She was away from Bruen; safe. Or was she?

Her eyes flickered to the driver.

Who was he? She didn't know him or recognize him yet he knew her name. Bruen didn't know her name. Had he truly rescued her then? He had appeared to have. But appearances could be deceiving her muddled brain told her. After all, there had been a faint trace of that foreign accent in his voice, hadn't there? She shuddered and edged closer to the door at the side of the van.

The man was driving with the assurance of one knowing where he was headed. He suddenly slowed the van to a more normal speed. Glancing back, he sent her a slight smile. "Come on up here," he said softly.

Casey shook her head.

"Please, Casey," he began, but his attention was diverted back to the road. He slowed and stopped for a traffic light, and Casey, without sparing him a second glance, was through the van's side door.

Chapter SIX

"Miss?"

Casey opened her eyes with a start.

"This is your stop."

She looked up at her apartment and sighed in relief. She was home. The children were safe. They would sit tight through the weekend and then with Donald's help...

She turned and managed to smile at the middle-aged taxi driver. "How much do I owe you?"

"$34.75," he told her.

Casey pulled what money she had from her pocket and counted it. "I'm afraid all I've got is twenty-three dollars, but if you'll wait I can run up and..."

"That's not necessary," the driver said with a quick smile. "Twenty-three dollars will be fine. You just go home and take care of yourself."

Casey didn't argue. She thanked him and made her way slowly up the apartment stairs to her door. She could hear the faint sound of the television and knew Chenin and Cortney were still up. She had hoped they would have been asleep.

She lifted the nearest flower pot from its dish and tore off the extra key she kept taped to the bottom of it. Bruen had given her no time to retrieve her keys from

Donald's car. She slid the key in the lock and it opened with a slight click.

Chenin was already running toward her. She threw her arms tightly around Casey. "Oh, T'Casey, you were so wonderful!"

Casey hardly heard the child as her eyes caught sight of the man sitting beside Cortney. It was impossible. She had left him driving a van near Lakeside and he had not followed her…

"It is all right, T'Casey," Cortney said, standing. "He is T'Keir. He is the son of Uncle Dajon."

The words didn't penetrate as the color drained from her face. After all she had gone through…

"Cortney, get her the tea." The man was across the room in seconds. "Come, Casey. It's best you sit down a moment." His voice was gentleness itself. Casey did not resist as he led her to the sofa. Chenin came, too, and planted herself on Casey's lap.

"T'Casey. You are crying," she said with a puzzled frown. "You must not. T'Keir is here now."

Casey hugged the child to her as her tears continued to fall.

Chenin was gently removed from her lap and Casey found Keir Jairon kneeling in front of her. He reached up and caressed her bruised cheek as his eyes apparently studied her. His voice was soft. "You are safe, Casey. You and Chenin and Cortney are safe."

A shuddered breath came out of her.

"T'Keir?" Chenin's voice was questioning.

"She will be fine, Chenin. She just needs a moment… Cortney?"

"I am coming."

Cortney came into the room balancing a steaming cup on a saucer. Keir took it from the boy and brought it up to Casey's lips. "Drink, Casey," he said gently. "Drink, and then we must go."

Casey drank, her tears blending with the hot liquid. She didn't want the tea, it was far too sweet, but Keir saw to it that she emptied the cup, and she was helpless to stop him.

He removed the cup and placed a feather light kiss on her warm lips. "Come, *sher'avi*. We best be going. I've taken the liberty to pack for you."

Casey looked at him blankly.

"We must leave," he said in the same quiet voice. "It will not be long before they, too, know where to come."

It was the steady hum of the motor that woke Casey. She was lying in a sleeping bag in a make-shift bed at the back of a camper van. The same van she had ridden in earlier, she realized. If only she had known; if only he had told her! She glanced around. Chenin and Cortney were asleep beside her in sleeping bags of their own. Keir Jairon, if indeed he was Keir Jairon, was at the wheel.

Quietly, so as not to wake the children, she slipped from the bed and up into the seat beside him to find it early morning.

"Are you all right, now?" Keir's voice was soft.

Casey nodded although her head and face still hurt and she felt heavy and drugged.

"There's aspirin in the glove box if you need them and I've got water here."

Casey fished out the aspirin then swallowed them with the water he had indicated. "Where are you taking us?"

"To my father." His glance was gentle. "Miss Hammond…"

"Casey."

"Casey." There was no title attached. "I am Keir Lael Jairon, son of Dajon Nal-Leal Jairon. Cortney and Chenin are my cousins."

"Can I see some identification?" she asked hesitantly, not wanting to take anything for granted anymore.

"Of course, *avi*."

Casey took the wallet handed to her and opened it; KEIR LAEL JAIRON; twenty-eight, six foot, blue eyes, brown hair. Her eyes went from the picture on the driver's license to his profile and back again. Yes, she noted, there definitely was a resemblance between him and his cousins despite his hair being a light brown instead of blonde. She closed the wallet. Her eyes closed as well, and she shivered.

"Cold, Casey?"

She shook her head feeling terribly tired. The air around her was cool, but not cold, the early morning sun having robbed it of its bite.

"Casey…"

"How did you know where to find them?"

Keir smiled faintly. "A she-bear never roams far from her cubs. You were running Casey, but you were running in circles, never more than an hour's drive of Saltine." His eyes met hers briefly. "When I found your wallet shoved under the seat of your car, I knew where they were."

Casey flushed. She had forgotten about the wallet. But when had he..?"

"I also removed your keys and the registration," he went on, "yesterday afternoon, when they followed you into the mall." His voice held question.

"I told them it was where I had left Chenin and Cortney."

"You also told them they were on a bus to Williamsport."

Casey's eyes flew to his.

"I was able to park the van beside their car. I had to know what they intended to do with you, and whether or not you handed Cortney and Chenin over to them." He stopped and shook his head. "You were convincing, Casey. Bruen believed you, but he did not trust you."

She shuddered. "I know. He wasn't…about to let me go."

"I know, *avi*. That is why I had to get you away from him." Keir grinned suddenly. "But you are a hard one to rescue T'Casey Hammond."

"I'm sorry."

"You have no need to be. I'm the one who should be sorry for frightening you so." A rueful smile came out of him. "I'm afraid I was too intent in getting you safely away to think of explaining my actions."

"I see." Not that it mattered any longer. She and Chenin and Cortney were safe now due to him. Her mind wandered to that silencing kiss realizing now that it had been just that, a way to protectively silence her.

"I take it you followed us to that motel?"

He nodded. "I wasn't about to leave you with Bruen and his men holding you. It took me awhile to realize that they had gotten two connecting rooms. Once Bruen left with one of his men, I took my chances in getting you out of there."

"Thank you." She was quiet a moment as her mind went over things. "The green and white Dodge?"

"Karl's car. He sent me after you the moment I arrived. I was in that taxi you narrowly missed. Your driving was...exceptional, Casey."

"I was scared silly." So it had been Keir who had pursued her to the old highway. His flashing headlights made sense now. Oh, if only she had known!

"Casey?" Keir's voice was hesitant, undecided, and it brought Casey's attention back to him. "Your car, it was registered to a Donald Hammond?"

"My cousin," she said. She flashed him a tired smile. "I was using his car while mine's in the shop being fixed. He's away on vacation at the moment." A tired, heavy breath escaped her. "Keir?"

"Yes?"

"You were there, at the mall?"

"Just two minutes behind you, Casey. After I had lost you that first time, I went back to Karl's. He assured me you would return. You did, but so unfortunately, did the nadarb. There was nothing I could do but follow; keep you in sight. Afraid of losing you inside the mall, I waited outside. Casey?" Again he was hesitant. "What did happen in there?"

"I got away...briefly."

"No wonder he was so angry."

Casey shuddered. "He had a gun."

"I know. Don't think about it, *avi*. As Chenin says, I am here now, and you are safe."

Casey swallowed and closed her eyes. "You're taking us to Washington?"

"Oregon. I borrowed the phone in your apartment to get in touch with my father. I owe you for that. I left a message for him to meet us at Turtle Sands, a small campground on the Oregon coast." He cast Casey a quick glance and fell silent. Her eyes remained closed and sleep was again over-taking her. She struggled against it.

"Karl Banning said you and your father moved to Washington."

"We did. Sleep now. We can talk later." His voice was gentle.

"But..."

"Hush."

"Keir..."

"Hush, Casey. No more talk."

Casey sighed, and her eyes closed...

Chapter **SEVEN**

It was quiet when she again woke. Peaceful. Her headache was just a dull ache and the side of her face only hurt when touched. She sat up and looked around. They were parked in a campground, one with trees everywhere. Cortney, Chenin, and Keir were tossing stones across a river, trying diligently to make them skip. Keir was exceptional at it, his every stone skipping nearly the entire breadth of the river. Casey yawned and watched them awhile without really watching.

Any doubts that she may have had against Keir had vanished. He was their protector now, and she was glad to leave it to him. A heavy breath suddenly escaped her. She had accomplished what she had begun, at least as nearly as possible. Keir was not Dajon Jairon, but that mattered little. He was the children's cousin. He was family, and her part in it all was over.

With a last glance at Keir and his cousins, she found her suitcase and headed for the large building in the center of the campground. It was a large enough building to accommodate showers, and if not, she would bathe in a sink.

Her first surmise proved correct and Casey took a long, soothing shower, staying until the water cooled. She changed into the clean clothes Keir had shoved into her suitcase and headed back to the van.

Keir and the children met her inside. The children, she noted absently, were each wearing a new t-shirt with the campground's logo on it. Keir's eyes came up and met hers. "Better?"

"Much better," she said, a flush staining her cheeks.

A warm smile came out of him. "Good. Then I can leave this to you." He apparently had been in the process of teaching Chenin how to use the small gas stove.

Amusement touched Casey. "You seem to be doing just fine."

"Ah, but it is not my place." Keir removed the suitcase from her hand and steered her toward the small stove.

Casey stopped in her tracks. "Keir Jairon! I suppose by that you mean it's *my* place, because I'm a woman?"

"Yes, because you are woman." His eyes sparked with amusement.

"Chauvinist!" Casey said indignantly. "I suppose you intend to keep your wife chained to the kitchen."

"As well as barefoot and pregnant," he said solemnly, attempting to smother a grin.

"You need to start living in the present century, Mr. Keir Jairon!"

A rich laugh came out of him.

"T'Keir, are you truly going to keep your wife chained to your kitchen?" Chenin was staring at him in disbelief.

Keir stooped down and hugged the child. "Of course not, *avi*. My wife will be in my kitchen because that is where she will want to be."

"I could be in your kitchen," the child said rather impulsively. "I could cook for you, and clean, and care for you, and..."

Keir kissed her lightly on the forehead. "No, little cousin. I believe my heart has already chosen another. But you may take care of this small home of ours while we are on the road if you choose."

"Oh, T'Keir. I choose!"

Keir grinned. "Then I suggest you ask Casey to teach you how to use the stove."

Casey did the unladylike thing and stuck her tongue out at him.

"Keir?"

"Hmm?"

Lunch was over, the van cleaned by Chenin's insistence, and Casey and Keir were sitting on the grassy bank of the river, watching the two children as they explored the riverbed. At least Casey was sitting. Keir was leaning lazily against a tree with his eyes closed. She bit her lip.

"Do you plan on traveling at night?"

"No," he said not bothering to open his eyes. "Last night was enough night traveling for one trip."

"How far do you think you'll get tomorrow?"

"We stay here tomorrow," he said absently. "Tomorrow is the Sabbath."

Surprise kept Casey silent for several long moments. It wasn't that she was anti-religious. She, herself, went to church regularly. But she could think of no one who honored the Sabbath outside of attending church. Religion however wasn't on her mind.

"Aren't you afraid of...of Bruen and the nadar, or what-ever it was Cortney called them, catching up with us and taking the children?"

Keir's eyes opened. "Relax," he said soothingly. "We are safe for the moment."

"How can you be so sure?" She wasn't sure at all.

He reached out and took her hand in his. "First, because at the moment, Bruen has no idea where we are and has no real way of finding out."

"And second?"

"They are likely already on their way to Washington."

"But..?"

"Having lost you yet again, there's no doubt they will have gone back to Karl," he said. "At the moment he is their only link to you, the children, and my father. Karl will willingly tell them we took the first flight to Seattle as well as turn over the Washington address I've given him that will lead them nowhere."

"What if they send the authorities after us? Put out an APB?"

His hand squeezed around hers. "It's not likely. Bruen will want to handle this as quietly as possible. He knows how severely he will be reprimanded if his superiors find he has let Chenin and Cortney slip away. They are rather important to their government at the moment."

"What makes them so important? They're only children."

"It is because they are the children of a scientist they are trying to control." Keir sat up, taking time to watch the children a moment before he turned to Casey. "How much has Cortney told you?"

"Very little. Only that his father was sending him and Chenin to live with your father. And that they, those men, would go to any lengths to see that they didn't escape." Casey's hand went unconsciously to her cheek where Bruen had struck her.

Keir nodded. "He is right, Casey. They would go to any lengths. They are the nadarb, Thern's secret police, a brutal secret organization run by the soviet government. Thern has been under their communistic rule now for twenty-eight years.

"My father and my uncle Davin, the children's father, were both schooled in America, and both scientists," Keir went on. "My father was attending a convention in the states when the communists invaded. Uncle Davin managed to wire him not to return, and in the upheaval, my mother was smuggled out and sent to my father."

"You were left in Thern?"

Keir smiled rather absently. "I am an American; conceived in Thern, but born in the States. That is why my mother was quickly smuggled out. Father would have otherwise returned to her, because of me."

"Your uncle didn't escape?"

"No. Uncle Davin was younger, and idealistic. He chose to stay until he could no longer help his countrymen. He was captured within weeks. They imprisoned him, and eventually, because of his profession, he was instructed to work. He has been working since."

Keir sighed and his eyes again rested on the two children playing in the distance. "Uncle Davin, their father, has made a scientific breakthrough. I am not sure exactly what. I am no scientist, but it has to do with fuel; atomic fuel, I think. The government has been pressuring him to complete his work. They would not hesitate to use his children's lives against him. He knows this. That is why he managed to send them both out of the country with a legal document giving Father life-custody of them both. But until they reach my father, they are still legally Davin's and belong to the controlling government. Our government would be powerless to stop them from taking the children back with them."

"But once your father has the papers, our government could legally prevent them from removing his children?"

"Yes."

Casey remembered how close they had come and shuddered. "But what's to prevent them from smuggling them back out anyway?"

Keir was silent so long that Casey began to think he hadn't heard. "Keir?"

His hand ran through his light brown hair. "Once he knows Cortney and Chenin have successfully escaped, Uncle Davin intends to…well, destroy all records and all concerned personnel, which includes himself. There will no longer be a need for his children after that."

Casey felt sick.

Keir went on quietly. "I don't understand the rest of the letter," but I'm sure my father will." He sighed and sank back against the tree once more.

Casey swallowed. "Do you think his children know?"

Keir's eyes went out to his two young cousins. "No, Casey. I doubt they know."

Casey's breath expelled.

"Do not dwell on it *avi*," Keir said softly, taking her hand again. He brought it up to his lips and kissed its knuckles.

Casey's heart jumped. She stared up at him, but his eyes were closed.

He was tired, Casey realized suddenly, which was no wonder considering he had driven all night and into the morning. He was also quite a man, she acknowledged. He had taken her and the children under his protection without so much as a thought. And it could not have been easy.

Her eyes roamed across his countenance, liking what she saw. Keir Jairon was definitely good-looking, she admitted. He was not an exceptionally big man, but he was solid, and there was a quiet, inner strength to him that instinctively commanded trust. He was also brave and intelligent and gentle and caring and…

She pulled her thoughts up short and looked out across the river. It would do no good to get emotionally involved with Keir Jairon. He had told Chenin his heart was already spoken for.

She glanced over at the two children. They were once again tossing stones across the river, quite as if they had not a care in the world. As if nothing had changed. Their father's bondage and his impending death did not exist for them. Maybe it was better.

"I'm going to hate leaving them," she said still watching Cortney and his sister. Already it was going to be difficult for they had a firm hold of her heartstrings.

Keir's eyes flew open. "You mustn't go yet, Casey."

"I have to," she whispered.

Keir sat up and turned her around to face him. "Have you forgotten the nadarb? They are dangerous men, Casey."

"They don't want me, Keir."

He gave her a slight shake. "Bruen has more than one score to settle with you, Casey. And he would never again believe that you do not know the whereabouts of the children. No." He slowly shook his head. "I cannot allow you to go yet."

"You cannot allow me?" Casey's temper flared. "It's my decision, Keir."

Keir's hand touched her bruised face, bringing back the pain. "Do you want more of that?" he asked quietly.

"No, but…" Tears sprang to her eyes. How could she explain it? How could she tell him that to stay would be just as dangerous, to her heart?

"Casey."

She stood up abruptly, intent on leaving, but stopped as she caught sight of Chenin running towards them. The girl was in tears.

"T'Casey! T'Keir! You must come!"

Casey's heart jumped. "What is it Chenin?"

The child threw herself at Keir and began a host of words in her native tongue.

"English, Chenin."

The girl gulped. "Cortney has lost his life-ring. It is not around his neck. Only his medallion is around his neck!"

Keir stood up immediately.

"What is it, Keir?"

"It's Cortney," he said, heading for the boy. "He's lost his life-ring."

Casey sent Keir a blank look then hurried to catch up with him. "He lost what?"

"His life-ring," Keir said without stopping. "A small ring he wears on a chain around his neck. The chain must have broken." He stopped as he reached the boy. "Where, Cortney?"

"I do not know," the boy said on a gulp.

"We were playing here," Chenin said with a gulp of her own, indicating the river's edge. "And there," she added pointing to another place nearby.

Keir immediately began to search. Casey knelt beside Cortney. "What was your ring like?"

The boy stood clutching the medallion still around his neck. "It is small…a silver-gold." He managed another gulp.

"About the size of a baby ring," Keir told her. Casey's eyes flew to his. To look for a ring that size along the river's edge would be like searching for the proverbial needle in the haystack. She turned back to Cortney. "You said there was a chain?"

"Yes," Cortney whispered. A single tear slid down his cheek, bringing a lump to Casey's throat.

She swallowed around it. "We'll find it, Cortney. It will be all right. We'll find it."

They didn't.

They searched until dusk but there was no sign of either the ring or the chain. Keir finally gathered them up.

"Come," he said. "It's too dark to keep looking. We'll look again when it's light."

Cortney and Chenin dejectedly obeyed their cousin, disappearing down the path toward the van. The two adults followed them more slowly.

"Keir?"

"I don't know, Casey." He sounded almost as dejected as Cortney had looked.

"Can't it be replaced?"

"It is part of him, Casey. It was given to him upon his birth as the symbol of his life." Keir stopped and took her hands. "You must understand, *avi*, to those of us from Thern, a life-ring is as important as one's wedding ring, if not more so. It stands for one's life and one's commitment to life…and eventually, for one's commitment to another as it is given freely in love."

"You exchange life-rings?"

"Yes." His eyes met hers.

Casey flushed and looked toward the two children. "Poor Cortney."

"I know. I suppose I should go talk to him." He sighed and glanced back at Casey. "Could you take Chenin?"

"She can help me find something for dinner."

Keir's hands squeezed hers. "Thank you, Casey."

Chapter EIGHT

Keir retrieved Cortney from the campsite and the two walked off together. Casey's heart went with them both. It was a devastating thing to lose something that held such personal value, and terribly difficult to console one who had.

"T'Casey?"

She looked down at Chenin. The girl still had tears in her eyes.

"It will be all right, Chenin."

"It is his life-ring," she whispered.

"I know." She knelt down beside the girl. "We must be brave for Cortney, Chenin. And be thankful that it is only his ring that is missing and not Cortney."

"We will look again for it tomorrow?"

"I promise."

She looked up into Casey's face. "You think…it will be found?"

"Yes, Chenin, I do," Casey lied stolidly, "but you must believe it, too."

Chenin took a deep breath. "Then I shall believe it, too."

"Good." Casey smiled and squeezed her hands. "Now, what do you say you and I run over to the lodge store and buying a bag of marshmallows to roast later?"

Interest flickered. "What are marshmallows, T'Casey?"

"Little pieces of white clouds, that melt sweetly and deliciously in your mouth." Casey bit back her grin.

Chenin looked at Casey in awe. "Truly?"

Casey laughed. "Well, almost." She stood and held out her hand. "Shall we go buy some and see?"

Chenin smiled tentatively. She took Casey's hand and together they left the van. Casey took her time buying more than just marshmallows, and by the time they returned with their purchases, Keir and Cortney were back and already had a blazing fire going. Chenin handed the package she carried to Casey and ran to join Keir and her brother. Casey followed more slowly.

"Very nice," she said commenting on the campfire as she joined them.

"Nice?" Keir cried mockingly, looking at his campfire. "It's more than nice. It's magnificent!"

"So it is," Casey said laughing up at him. It was good to see a smile on his face again, and Cortney, too, looked a little happier. "Did you happen to save any branches long enough to roast marshmallows?"

He grinned. "You mean little white clouds that turn golden and warm and delicious in the flames?"

Casey flushed.

"I've got several put aside, Casey."

"Good thing you do!"

Keir merely laughed.

Casey slipped into the van and began cooking a light, quick dinner that both children eagerly downed in order to experience the new adventure of roasting marshmallows. Keir got the sticks ready and after the flames had turned to burning coals, Chenin and Cortney had their first lessons in roasting the sweet treats. And, as with all beginners, their marshmallows burned.

"Cortney, your marshmallow!"

Cortney quickly drew his burning marshmallow from the fire and blew out the flame. He looked unhappily to Keir.

Keir grinned. "Try eating it anyway. You'll be surprised."

Cortney was. After one tentative bite, he stuffed the rest into his mouth and reached for another. From then on, it did not bother him one way or another whether his marshmallows burned, although he did admit they were best when roasted to a golden brown.

Both children stuffed themselves. "I am so full," Cortney said at last, bringing his dinner plate to Casey after having given Keir his stick. He reached up and kissed her on the cheek. "Thank you, T'Casey, for the supper, and for the marshmallows!"

Chenin was right behind him. She, too, kissed Casey on her cheek. "Thank you, T'Casey." She picked up the plates on Casey's lap. "I will take these inside."

Casey sat where she was, savoring the contentment invading her. She was hardly aware of Keir moving until his lips suddenly brushed hers in a soft kiss.

"Jairon tradition," he murmured. "Always kiss the cook." His eyes held a mischievous twinkle.

Casey blushed deeply and turned away. "Chenin did as much as I did."

A rumbled laugh came out of him. "Then I suppose I had better go kiss her as well." He stood and disappeared after Chenin.

Casey stood up and poked at the embers, her face still hot. She felt unaccountably light. Because Keir Jairon had kissed her? She shook her head, pushing the thought away. No. It was more likely because she was here.

She glanced around at the trees that were no more than dark shapes and breathed in their pine scent. The sky was dimming from gray to black and she could even see the twinkling of several early stars. A sigh of contentment came out of her. She loved camping in the mountains. She always had.

Her glance came around as Chenin and Cortney returned followed by their cousin. Keir began to try and to teach them several campfire songs in English, sending them all into giggles. Yet, despite the gayety, Cortney's light mood slowly vanished and Casey found him once again looking forlorn and unhappy as he fingered for the chain that was no longer there.

Her eyes rested on the medallion still around his neck. Why couldn't it have been the one to break loose? Why did it have to be the boy's precious life-ring?

Coming to her feet, she disappeared quietly into the van to prepare the beds. There were only two; one in the front of the van above the two seats, and a larger one in the back formed by the lowering of the table. Although the one at the back was big enough to hold the two children's sleeping bags, and one for her, she refused to consider it necessary. Chenin would sleep with her; Cortney with Keir.

Neither child seemed to mind when she told them and put them to bed and Keir did not comment on it at all. He said his good-nights to both his cousins reminding them to say their prayers and then joined Casey by the fireside.

"Tired?" he asked as he settled himself down on the log beside her.

"Not really."

"How's your headache?"

"It's actually gone." She fiddled with the stick in her hand a moment then tossed it into the cooling embers. "Are you really going to just stay here tomorrow?"

"Yes, Casey. We'll be staying. As I said, tomorrow is the Sabbath."

"But what about getting Chenin and Cortney to your parents as soon as possible?"

"There's no need for us to rush, Casey," he said. "We have time to get to Oregon. My parents have a ways to come in order to meet us there."

"Why in Oregon and not in Washington? He lives in Washington, doesn't he?"

Keir glanced at her. "He does, but at the moment, he and my mother are at a scientific convention overseas. I thought it best we avoid waiting for them anywhere near home while they are in transit. There's always the chance Bruen will be able to find my or my parent's address before my parents can get to us."

It did made sense Casey admitted. "So you wired them to meet us in Oregon."

"Actually I phoned but was unable to talk to either parent, so I left a message."

"My phone wasn't the cause, was it?"

His head shook. "There was some static but that was most likely due to it being an overseas call. The call went through. It's just neither of my parents were available."

"I see. How long do you think it will take them to get home?"

"I really expect them to arrive about the same time we do, but it just depends on how things go on their end. They could be back on Monday or as late as maybe Wednesday."

"I see."

Keir's hand slipped into hers. "Don't worry about it, Casey. They'll meet us in the campground in Oregon as soon as they possibly can."

"It's a shame they can't just meet us here," she said. She hated the thought of having to travel all the way to Oregon.

"A tad too close to Salt Lake City," he said lightly. "Though I know what you mean. I love being here in the mountains. I love the quiet up here, the fresh smell of the pine-scented air; the sound of the wind through the trees."

"And the stars that are so bright and so close you feel you can reach up and touch them," Casey added looking up at the star-studded night sky.

Keir grinned. "Yes. That, too. Do you go camping much, Casey?"

"Not anymore," she said. "Our family used to, from time to time. We used to go from campground to campground when we traveled across country to visit relatives." She grinned suddenly and a soft laugh came out of her. "I can remember my parents taking us one year with snow still on the ground. My brothers, well, Don and Henry that is, teased me terribly that summer. They had convinced me that Bigfoot was roaming about disguised as the abominable snowman. They had me so terrified that I had been afraid to go anywhere by myself." She giggled at the memory. "Poor guys. They had me stuck to them like glue through that whole vacation."

"How old were you?"

"A gullible nine year old."

"You must have been cute."

"Yeah, right." Casey shook her head. "I was a big tomboy back then. I did everything my brother and my cousin did. Or, at least I tried to. We did a lot of fishing and hiking in those days. I think they used to try and tire me out so I would leave them in peace, but I had more energy than they did."

"They teach you how to fish?"

"No. Our father did. But it was something we all enjoyed doing, that, and hiking...and star gazing." She glanced up at the stars and took a deep breath of the pine-scented air. "I hadn't realized how much I missed it until now."

"Then you should enjoy this next week," he said lightly.

Casey's eyes flew to his. "Keir..."

"Hush," he whispered, bringing his fingers to her lips. "Casey, I ask only that you help me watch over Chenin and Cortney until I can turn them over to my parents." He removed his fingers and his lips touched hers in a gentle kiss.

"Please, think on it, *avi*. You see, we need you, Chenin and Cortney and I, very, very much."

75

Casey was up at dawn the next day. It was clear and blue and crisp. And quiet. The river was scattered with fishermen but even they did not interrupt the solitude of the early morning. It was perfect.

Too perfect to be thinking of leaving, or of staying. Casey pushed both thoughts from her mind. She refused to admit that her mind was already decided.

"Natahahn, sher'avi."

The greeting startled Casey and she would have fallen into the river had not Keir caught her. "I'm sorry. I didn't realize you were so deep in thought."

She resettled herself back on the rock where she had been sitting. *"Natahahn sher'avi* – is that good morning?"

"Good morning, good night, hello, good bye. *Natahahn* is basically a general greeting among friends."

"I take it you were taught the Thernian language."

"Not actually," he said as he settled himself on the rock beside her. "I've picked up some, but on a whole, no, I grew up speaking English…You're up early."

"I woke early. Are the kids still asleep?"

"No. Chenin's attempting to make breakfast and Cortney is supervising."

Casey sent him a sour look. "I suppose it isn't his place to help."

Keir grinned.

"I'm sorry for your future wife."

"Woman was created for man, Casey."

"Right. To be enslaved, and used, and discarded?"

"No." His hands came up gently and cradled her face and she found herself looking up into his warm, blue eyes. His voice was gentle. "A woman, Casey, is to be loved, and needed, and cherished beyond all else."

Familiar balming sweetness began invading her and she quickly pulled her eyes away. "Tell me about her, Keir, your future wife, what is she like?"

His eyes were warm as they lazily roamed across her; his was voice tender. "Ah, Casey, she's wonderful; so warm and caring. She's intelligent and brave and funny, and... softhearted. Sometimes stubborn and quick-tempered," he added with a slight grin, "but I'm finding her always a joy."

"Is she beautiful?"

The grin spread to a warm smile as his eyes rested again on her. "Yes, Casey," he said softly. "She's beautiful, and the most desirable woman I have ever known."

Casey smiled, vaguely aware of the depression that was beginning to settle within her. "Will you be married soon?" she made herself ask.

A light breath escaped him. "It is too soon to ask her."

Too soon or was he too nervous? She dismissed the question for she could not see Keir Jairon nervous of anything or anyone. Nor could she see any woman turning him down. He was everything one could want in a man; good-looking, intelligent, solid, yet warm and sensitive…and devoted to the one he loved.

She pulled her thoughts up short. "I suppose I should go and see how Chenin is getting along."

"Don't," Keir said softly, putting out a hand. "She wants very much to do this one on her own. It's her way of expressing her thanks to the both of us."

"They made me breakfast yesterday morning."

"I know. They told me." He was quiet a moment. "Would you tell me something?"

She looked questioning at him.

"What made you decide to take Chenin and Cortney under your wing?"

Casey shrugged. "They…needed me. They were two scared, lonely kids in a country not their own. The authorities would only have terrified them further. And I couldn't see abandoning them. Besides, they wanted only to get to your father and that supposedly was only a short forty minute drive away. I never expected…" She stopped and swallowed.

"I'm sure you didn't. You know, I haven't yet thanked you for what you've done for them. I don't quite know how."

"You saved my life," she reminded him uncomfortably. She didn't want thanks. It was enough that she and the children were safe.

Keir found her hand and gave it a light squeeze and a companionable silence fell between them. Casey, her hand still in Keir's, sat comfortably watching the river and soaking up the early morning sun. She was at peace for the first time since her brother had decided to get married.

Keir did not invade her peace; he was part of it, sitting beside her in quiet understanding.

"T'Keir?" It was Cortney. "Breakfast is prepared if you and T'Casey are ready to eat."

"We are ready." Keir slipped down and helped Casey from the rock. They both followed Cortney back to the van.

Casey was impressed. Chenin served them a skillet of scrambled eggs mixed with diced onion, tomatoes, bell peppers, and ham. It was topped with cheese and served with toast and milk.

"Chenin, this is wonderful!"

Chenin beamed. "You must thank T'Keir as well, for he had everything cut already."

The man grinned as Casey flashed him a look.

"But Chenin put it all together and cooked it," Cortney said with so much pride that Casey stared at him in surprise. Her eyes went to Keir.

"The men of Thern are proud of their women," he said. His eyes were sparkling.

"I guess." She looked at him seriously. "Do they all start cooking, like this, so young?"

"The culinary arts begin at age five, for all children," he answered.

"The male species as well?"

A laugh rumbled out of him. "Yes, the male species as well. Cortney and I both cook, out of enjoyment, or out of necessity. But," he added with a teasing light, "Neither of us would ever interfere with a woman's rightful position."

Casey's liberated views sprang to the top and she frowned darkly.

"You do not like to cook?" Chenin sounded surprised.

"I love to cook," Casey smiled at the child. She cast a glance at Keir. "It's the 'rightful position' I object to."

Chenin looked at her blankly and Keir leaned over and whispered something to her. Both children turned astonished eyes on Casey.

Casey looked accusingly to Keir. "What on earth did you tell them?"

"Only that you do not feel that it is important to be a woman."

"It's important to be who you are!"

"Yes," he said with a warm smile, "and you are woman."

"I am a person!" Casey retorted.

Keir's eyes met hers. "Oh, Casey. Everyone is a person. But you, you are so much more. You are a woman; warm and tender and loving. You're the mother of humanity, Casey, the necessity of man. And without you, we could not exist."

He reached over and touched her face. "Understand," he said softly, "you are the most precious part of man, more precious than any gold, or silver, or diamond; precious, because you *are* a woman."

A multitude of conflicting feelings ran through Casey. "It still doesn't give a man the right to chain his wife to the house," she whispered.

"There are no chains, Casey. A wife is there because she gives 100% of herself to her husband. His life, his home, his children become the most important things in her life. It is the love of a woman, Casey."

"Chauvinist!" she muttered.

Keir laughed softly. He looked toward the children. "I think it's time we gave Casey her peace."

"We will look for my life-ring?"

"Just until worship, Cortney."

"And after?"

"And afterwards, if it's necessary." He looked back up at Casey. "They give a worship service in the meadow, if you feel up to it."

"Thanks." She picked up a handful of breakfast dishes. "Now, if you'll just *excuse* me."

A soft laugh came out of him. He motioned to the children and with a kiss, they disappeared out of the van.

"Chauvinist!" Casey muttered again.

Casey cleared the small table, washed up the breakfast dishes, then straightened up the rest of the van. She really didn't mind the work, but because it was something she wanted to do to show her thanks, not because it was her rightful position. No, definitely not because it was her rightful position!

"T'Casey?"

She turned to find Chenin in the van. "What is it, Chenin?"

"It is time for worship. T'Keir asks that you come, if you will. And bring his Bible. Will you come, T'Casey?" The girl looked to her with hopeful eyes.

Casey smiled. "I'll come. I think your cousin's Bible is on the dash, up front."

Chenin retrieved the Bible and the two of them went out to find Keir and Cortney waiting. Together they joined the other campers for the outside worship service. The meadow was bright with sunshine and peaceful; the river running gently by. It was the perfect place to hold service.

It was a quiet and simple service, and Casey again marveled at the peace; a peace that she had desperately needed she realized as she lay back into the grass after the service.

Bliss; to do nothing…to think nothing.

Casey heaved a deep, contented sigh and opened her eyes. Keir was sitting quietly beside her on the gently sloping hillside of the meadow.

"Have a nice nap?"

"I wasn't sleeping," she said stretching comfortably.

"No?" He laughed softly.

The laugh brought Casey up. "Just how long have you been sitting there?"

He shrugged. "About an hour. I didn't want to disturb you. You've needed this."

"I suppose I have, especially with my brother's wedding and everything else that's happened." She smiled and glanced around. "I can't believe it's so peaceful here. Have you come here often, Keir?" He seemed so at home in the campground, as if he had been here many times before.

"A few times," he said. "Though our family's hideaway is now a small campground called Raccoon Creek up in the Smoke River Mountains." He smiled at Casey. "My father has a passion for camping."

"That he seems to have passed onto his son."

Keir grinned, but continued. "When I was small, we camped almost everywhere, including here. Then Father found Raccoon Creek. That was it; his paradise on Earth. I doubt if he's been camping anywhere else since."

"Does he go often?"

"Whenever he can get away or whenever he's got a serious problem he needs to think about. It's his escape. Retreat, I think it's called. Thankfully, by moving to Washington, he's actually closer to it now."

Casey frowned as she thought about it. "But instead of meeting him there, we're meeting him on the Oregon coast?"

Keir shrugged. "Safer that way. Too many know of his ties to Raccoon Creek so there's a possibility that someone who knows of it may accidently let the name slip. On the flip side, neither Dad nor I have any ties to Turtle Sands which means Bruen and his cohorts are not likely to even contemplate it as a possible location."

"I see what you mean."

Keir laid back. Casey bit her lip.

"You tired?"

"Just lazy," he said. He reached up and pulled her down with him. "Tell me about yourself, Casey. Have you always lived near Salt Lake City?"

Her head shook. "Actually, I was born in Chicago and then raised in California. Donald and I moved to Saltine when Henry was transferred there."

"Are your parents still living in California?"

"No...They died two years ago in a plane crash."

"I'm sorry," Keir said softly. He turned on his side and tactfully changed the subject. "Is Henry your only brother?"

"In actual fact, but Donald has lived with us since he was four. He's as much a brother to me as Henry."

"I sort of gathered that. You seem to count on him."

Casey looked at him in confusion. "I do. He, Henry, and I have always been close; more so as we have gotten older. How did you know?"

"You told Cortney to call your cousin if you didn't make it back to your apartment."

"Something I should have done before I put myself in that predicament," she said wryly. "It would have been a long wait though. Donald's not due back until tonight." She shook her head. "I don't think I could have waited that long."

"No boyfriend you could have turned to?" Lightly.

Casey shook her head again. She had a few male friends and she dated semi-regularly, but there was no one special. No one she could have counted on. "Keir? Would you have..?"

"I would have waited, Casey, or have found you somehow; you and the children." His hand gently reached out and caressed her cheek. "I wasn't about to leave without you."

Casey flushed and sat up. She felt light-headed and vulnerable and knew without a doubt she was heading for dangerous ground. She turned her attention to the two children.

"They're still at it," she said, watching Chenin and Cortney searching the riverside for Cortney's lost ring. They had searched all morning before worship without success and now they were at it again. Keir sat up beside her.

"Keir?"

"Hmm?" His eyes, too, were on the children.

"What happens if he can't find it?"

"I don't know, Casey. I've never lost mine." He stood and pulled her to her feet. "Let's go take them on a hike. It may take their minds off their troubles."

"I hope so," Casey said, doubting it. The children were too concerned about Cortney's ring to let a hike divert them for long. She followed Keir regardless as he gathered his two cousins.

Chapter TEN

Together they headed for the path leading through the trees; Chenin, with her hand in Casey's, and Cortney, with his in Keir's.

"You will not get us lost, will you, T'Keir?"

"No, Chenin," Keir said with a grin. "I won't get us lost."

Cortney cast a forlorn look back toward the river. "Where are we going to?" There was no enthusiasm in his voice.

"This way," Keir said. "If I remember correctly, there should be a waterfall not too far from here."

Chenin's hand tightened around Casey's. "What is a waterfall?"

Casey dimpled. "Wait and see."

Keir led them up through the trees, starting a contest to see which child could find the most living things. It was a science lesson Casey as well as the children thoroughly enjoyed for Keir willingly told them something about all they could point out.

"But where is the waterfall to be found?" Chenin asked after a while.

"I'm not sure," Keir said, bringing them to a standstill. "I guess my memory isn't what it used to be."

Chenin looked up at Casey. "Does that mean we are lost?"

"It means the waterfall is lost," Keir said before Casey could reply.

Casey grinned at him. "Shouldn't the river be over that way?"

"The river turns, or at least it used to." Keir glanced around then turned back to Casey. "Do you still want to go on?"

She shrugged. "Why not? Chenin says she hasn't seen a waterfall."

"That is not so," Cortney said immediately. He said something to his sister in their own tongue and she nodded. "Well, that is a waterfall."

"Oh. Will it be bigger?"

Keir grinned. "Why don't we find out?"

The waterfall was bigger Chenin informed them when they finally found it. Much bigger. They stood at the edge of the river watching it cascade over the top and pound resoundingly into the water before them.

"It is very...loud, is it not?" Chenin said, not taking her eyes from the waterfall.

"It is, rather," Casey said with a warm smile to the girl.

The child shivered and moved closer to Casey. "T'Casey. I do not like it."

Casey bent down and picked her up. "It's all right, Chenin," she said hugging her. She shot a glance at Keir then smiled again at Chenin. "Why don't we leave these two to their waterfall and see what we can find along the river."

"All right," Chenin said in obvious relief. She brightened. "Maybe we will find Cortney's life-ring."

"Maybe." Casey put Chenin down, took her hand, and together they walked slowly along the riverbank in the direction of camp, leaving Cortney and Keir to their own devices.

The waterfall eventually disappeared from sight and Chenin visibly relaxed once the waterfall was only an echo in their ears. She began concentrating once again on finding Cortney's ring.

Casey warned the girl twice to be careful as she peered over the edges of the riverbank. It was a two-to-four foot drop in places, and although there did not appear to be any rocks in the shallow water, the current itself looked unpredictable.

"I am careful, T'Casey." The girl hunted a moment or two longer for Cortney's ring then gave up and joined Casey. They walked along quietly for several minutes in the coolness of the trees that banked the river. "T'Casey?"

"What is it, Chenin?"

The girl glanced up at her. "The stove in Uncle Dajon's van, does it bake pies?"

"I believe so," Casey said with a touch of surprise. Would the two Thernian children ever cease to amaze her? "You would like to bake a pie, Chenin?"

The girl nodded. "Yes, I want to bake a pie for T'Keir. Can I bake one for him?"

"I don't see why not. Any special kind?"

Chenin skipped beside her. "Oh, any kind. He said to me he likes them all."

Mud pies as well? Casey grinned wryly, wondering when Chenin had managed to extract such information from her cousin. "We'll have to wait until we can stop at a store though," she said. "Will that be all right?"

"Is not the lodge a store?"

"It is, but it really doesn't have what we need. Why don't we…"

Casey's words died in her throat as out of nowhere, two large bodies dropped from the trees above, almost on top of them. Casey heard Chenin scream as she pushed the girl out of the way, only to scream herself as she tripped backwards and felt herself tumble down the bank of the river and into the water below.

"T'Casey!"

"Lady?"

Casey heard Chenin call out her name once more. She slowly righted herself, trying to adjust to where she was. She was wet and cold, but she wasn't hurt. The riverbank had been soft and the water where she sat was only a foot or so deep. Mud, she was sure, was running down her temples.

"Lady, are you okay?"

Casey turned and looked up to find Chenin and two hefty teenage boys staring down at her in concern, and then from behind them, Cortney and Keir.

Casey groaned as the look of concern on Keir's face turned to amusement as he assessed her.

"Casey? Are you all right?"

He was actually laughing at her! She glared up at him. "Do I look all right?"

"Actually," he said as a warm chuckle came out of him, "you look a little comical sitting there."

"Thanks!" she muttered, throwing water up in his direction. He stood there grinning as she climbed to her feet and surveyed the disaster.

"Come on, Casey," Keir said, holding out his hand to her.

With another disgusted glance at herself, Casey threw her hand into his and let him pull her up the embankment.

"We're really sorry, lady," the first teenager said. "We didn't mean to scare you like that."

"We just sort of fell," said the other.

"I just sort of fell," Casey stated. "You two just sort of dropped."

"I guess we did." Both looked unhappily at her.

"You guess you did what?" A woman appeared looking concerned and not very patient. Both teenagers groaned as the older woman hurried to join them.

"It was an accident, Mom. Honest!"

Their mother wasn't listening. She was surveying Casey's soaking, mud-spattered countenance.

"Oh, goodness. My boys did this to you?"

"Actually, I did most of it myself," Casey said wryly. She cast a look at the two boys. "Not that they didn't help a bit."

"What did happen?" Keir was looking at them curiously.

The boys shifted their feet uncomfortably. "We... well, we were playing in the trees," one said.

"And we...well, we fell out of this one practically on top of her," said the other.

"And I tripped getting out of their way and ended in the river," Casey finished the dialog. "End of story."

"You forgot to say that you pushed me down, T'Casey," Chenin said.

Laughter bubbled forth. "I did, didn't I? I'm sorry, Chenin. Are you all right?"

Chenin nodded. "But you look awful, T'Casey."

"I guess I do." Casey looked down and surveyed herself again. She looked up to find Keir watching her, amusement in his eyes.

"I guess I had better get you out of those wet clothes."

Casey flushed as the simple thought of Keir doing just that sent warm shivers throughout her. He didn't mean it; she knew that, but...

"Cold, Casey?"

Her flush deepened as she caught the warm laughter in his voice. He knew, darn him! He knew what he was doing to her!

"Oh, please," the boys' mother interrupted them in misunderstanding, "Take my sweater. You must be freezing in this breeze, and I would feel awful if you caught cold."

Casey shivered, surprised to realize she was cold. She hadn't noticed the breeze, not with Keir's teasing, but she felt it now. She reached out for the sweater offered, but Keir was there first.

"You really are cold, aren't you?" he said, wrapping the sweater around her shoulders. Concern had replaced the laughter.

The lady looked rather threatening at her two boys. "I think you've got a lot to answer for as well as some major apologizing to do."

The boys mumbled another apology and disappeared down the path. "I really am sorry," the boys' mother told Casey again. "I really don't know what gets into them at times. I hope you're really all right?"

"I'm sure I will be," Casey said trying not to shiver.

"Well, I can guarantee those two won't be when I get finished with them." With another shake of her head she headed after her boys.

Keir shook his head then turned to Chenin and Cortney. "Come on you two, we best get Casey into some dry clothes."

It was a faster walk, going back to camp, to which Casey was very thankful for. The breeze was cool and she was cold and shivering despite the sweater and wanted nothing more than to get into a hot shower.

But even that didn't seem to help. Though the shower and dry clothes felt good, Casey still felt chilled. Would she catch cold? She hoped not. She couldn't afford to be sick, not with Chenin and Cortney's safety to worry about.

She picked up her wet clothes and dripping shoes, and headed back to the van, relieved to find Keir had a fire already going. He took the wet clothes from her and handed them to Chenin.

"Feeling any better?"

"Yes," Casey lied.

"You don't look it."

Casey sighed and held out her shoes to him. "It would help to have dry shoes."

"Go get warm," he said indicating the fire. Casey didn't need to be told twice. She sat by the fire and watched as Chenin diligently hung up the wet clothes to dry. Keir placed her tennis shoes near the fire then peeled off the sweater he was wearing and handed it to her.

"I've got another one in the van," he said when she hesitated.

"It wouldn't matter if you didn't." Casey took the sweater and slipped it over her head, glad for the added warmth.

Keir grinned then glanced down at her bare feet. "I'll get you some socks." He disappeared into the van. He was back a moment later, tossing a pair of his thick, heavy socks at her. "Here. Wear them in health." He slipped another sweater over his head and motioned to Cortney.

Casey's heart jumped. "Keir?"

"You stay put. Cortney and I are going to see if we can gather some more wood before it gets any darker."

Casey sighed as she watched them disappear. She moved closer to the fire, adding several more branches to it. It blazed brightly for a few minutes as it quickly consumed the added timber, then died down again.

"T'Casey?"

She looked up at Chenin.

"T'Keir has tea for you, if you are ready for it."

"I'd love some, Chenin."

She grinned as the girl disappeared into the van. Tea seemed to be the cure-all of the Jairon family. Actually, it wasn't such a bad cure-all Casey acknowledged a few minutes later as Chenin handed her a steaming mug. It was hot, and Casey sipped it gratefully.

Feeling somewhat warmer at last, her thoughts turned to food. "I guess we had better find something for supper."

"There is no need," said Chenin. "T'Keir said we were to cook something in the fire tonight. Frank tuffers?"

Casey laughed at the confused look on the girl's face. "Frankfurters, Chenin. Actually, we call them hot dogs. They're long strips of meat, sort of like sausages. We put them on sticks and roast them in the flames like we did the marshmallows last night."

"Are they good?" She sounded dubious.

"Are what good?" Cortney had joined them. He dropped an armful of wood and repeated his question.

"Hot dogs," said his sister.

Cortney looked shocked. "You eat dogs?"

Casey fought down a giggle. "No. That's just a nickname we've given them. They're actually pork or beef."

Both children looked relieved. Casey turned to Keir as he came up behind them. "If you get them started on the hot dogs, I'll see what I can find to go with them."

Keir dropped his handful of wood on top of Cortney's. "Are you implying, Casey Hammond, that you don't trust my good culinary abilities?"

Casey flushed. "What I'm implying is that I'm hungry!" she said with a huff.

He grinned. "Patience."

Casey had no choice. Keir took his time preparing bacon and beans and heating the buns before they were allowed to start on the hot dogs. But it was worth the wait she thought later as she sat back watching Chenin and Cortney's happy faces as they finished off the last of them. They had enjoyed the hot dogs almost as much as they had enjoyed the marshmallows.

Chenin, full at last, put her roasting stick down and kissed her cousin. "Thank you, T'Keir. It was so good!"

"I'm glad you enjoyed it," he said, accepting a kiss from Cortney as well. He turned mischievous eyes to Casey.

She flushed. "You told me to stay put."

"Oh, I can take care of that." He moved from his log to hers. "Is this better?"

"Yes," she said, surprising him as she planted a warm kiss on his cheek. "Thank you, cook."

Chenin tapped his leg. "T'Keir, is it a long way to Uncle Dajon?"

"I'm afraid it is, *avi*," he replied poking the fire.

"Will it take many days?"

Keir shook his head, tossing the stick he held into the flames. "We'll be there by tomorrow evening, Chenin."

"We are to leave tomorrow?" There was panic in Cortney's voice.

"We must, Cortney."

"But T'Keir!" he cried, "My life-ring. We have not found it!"

"I know." Keir's voice was gentle, but there was a firmness about it, too. He bent and took the boy's hands. "You must not worry, Cortney. Someone will find it, and we'll leave our address so they know where to send it."

The boy took a deep steadying breath and hugged his cousin.

Casey sighed and headed for the van. Her feet were freezing and she was beginning to shiver again. And, she was tired. She slipped a second pair of Keir's heavy socks on and made herself another hot cup of tea before she began preparing the beds.

"T'Casey!"

Cortney came charging into the van. "T'Keir is taking us into the lodge. Will you come, too?"

Casey smiled, but shook her head. "I don't think so, Cortney."

He charged back outside and a moment later Keir appeared at the door.

"Casey?" He glanced at the beds. "Are you turning in?"

"I thought I might."

He eyed the cup of tea. "You still cold?"

She nodded.

"There's a clean sweat suit in my suitcase. Maybe you'd better wear it tonight."

"Thank you," she said sincerely, then, "Are you really going to leave your address at the lodge?" Concern laced her voice.

He shrugged. "Who knows? It might actually show up."

"Isn't it dangerous though, Keir?" It had bothered her from the moment Keir had first suggested it. It wasn't likely Bruen would be able to trace them to the campground, but it was possible. Anything was possible.

"Not when it's your address," Keir said with a wry shrug. "Look, I'll dampen the fire a bit before we go. You get some rest."

Her heart jumped. "Keir?"

He stopped and looked up questioning. She flushed and shook her head, not certain why she had stopped him.

"Sleep well, Casey," he said softly.

"I will." She watched as he disappeared out the door. With a heavy sigh, she finished the beds, found Keir's sweat suit, and changed.

Trust him to have anything and everything on hand, she thought as she slipped into her sleeping bag. Not that she minded, she admitted, savoring the extra warmth. She curled deeper into the bag wondering if he had ever been a boy scout, but her eyes closed and she was asleep…

Chapter ELEVEN

I t was hours, but it seemed only minutes later, that her eyes flew open; her every nerve screaming silent warnings. She lay without moving in the darkness, listening. She didn't know what it was that woke her, but her heart was pounding and she knew something was not right. What?

She strained her ears. She could hear Chenin's gentle breathing; hear Keir's heavier breathing across the van…A car on the highway…

And then she heard it again, the soft tread of feet on the gravel outside; the quiet sound of metal grating against metal. Her heart jumped. Bruen?

It couldn't be! Could it? But she was already slipping silently out of the sleeping bag.

She made her way to Keir and shook him, gently at first, then harder, afraid to call out his name. He shifted positions, but did not wake.

"Keir!" Her voice was just a breath as she shook him again, even harder yet. He opened his eyes this time and he looked blankly up at her.

"Case?"

Her hand covered his mouth. "There's someone outside the van," she whispered shakily.

Keir froze momentarily as his eyes met hers, and then he slowly removed her hand from his mouth. He didn't let go and she felt his fingers tighten around hers. He had heard it, too. He slipped out of his sleeping bag and into his jeans, pulling on his shoes.

"Keir?" Her heart was still pounding painfully against her chest.

"Hush," he whispered, pulling his keys from his pocket and shoving them at her. "If I give the order, you get out of here. Fast. Head for Turtle Sands."

He grabbed his hunting knife from the counter and slipped quietly out of the side door before Casey could protest.

She stared after him a moment, then almost in afterthought, locked the door. She looked anxiously out the small window above the sink but could see nothing. And, at first, she heard nothing; not even Keir's shoes on the gravel.

But then it came; the clang of something hitting the van and the scuffle of feet. She heard flesh hitting flesh, groans…and then nothing.

Keir? Casey listened apprehensively at the window, but there was nothing. Just silence. A minute ticked by… then two. She cautiously slid into the cab of the van and peered out its window. Keir was standing some twenty feet away, staring in the direction of the trees, apparently unhurt.

Casey's heart jolted in relief. She slipped out of the van and made her way to him.

"Keir?"

He shot her a look. "It's all right. They're gone."

She swallowed. "Do you think they were..?"

"I don't think so, Casey," he said, his eyes still on the trees, "but I don't think we'd better take any chances."

She eyed him nervously, not liking the sound of that. "Keir?"

He turned and gave her a gentle shove in the direction of the van. "Go get your shoes on."

"They're still wet." Why didn't he say what he meant?

"Dry enough, so go put them on, and get the flashlights."

Casey did as she was told, putting on her damp shoes, muttering as she did so. It was easier to vent anger in Keir's direction than to think about the dangerous possibilities that still existed. She found the flashlights and joined Keir again. He was at the back of the van, running his hands over the cold metal.

"Thanks." He took one of the flashlights from her and turned back to the van. "Look for anything that doesn't belong," he said, running his hands over the cold metal once more.

"You think they put something on the van?"

"I think," he said, stopping long enough to shoot her a look, "They were just after the spare tire. I just want to be sure."

She trained her eyes on the van. "What are we looking for?"

"Anything that could be a transmitter."

It was Casey's turn to shoot him a look. "A transmitter?"

"Tracking devices. The nadarb are known for their use of them." He continued with his quick, thorough check of the van. Casey, with an uneasy breath, did the same.

They found nothing. Keir sent her a smile filled with relief. "Well, that's that."

"What now?" Casey asked flicking off her flashlight.

Almost immediately a flash of light shone on them both. "Got a problem?"

They both swung around, but it was only the manager of the lodge.

Keir shook his head. "Not now. We were just getting ready to pull out."

Casey shot him a surprised, nervous look, but said nothing. She wasn't averse to leaving. On the contrary, she preferred it after the night's events. But the fact that Keir was so ready to leave made her more uneasy than ever. Was he still unsure?

The manager moved closer. "If you're sure everything's all right?"

Keir nodded, giving Casey a gentle shove toward the van. She took the hint, leaving him to put the manager's mind to rest as she began gathering her still damp clothes and the other odds and ends that had been left outside the van. Her mind, however, was still with Keir. It was several minutes before he joined her.

"Did you tell him?"

Keir nodded. "Apparently they've had a lot of thefts around here lately."

"You think that's all it was?"

"I do." He shot her a smile. "Why don't you get those into the van and move Cortney while I check the water and oil."

Fifteen minutes later Casey found herself in the front seat of the van as it headed onto the highway and toward the west coast. Keir didn't appear in any hurry, and so with another reassuring glance at the two sleeping children, she settled back. Keir shot her a glance.

"You didn't mind leaving, did you?"

Casey shook her head. "No."

"Good. I thought it was crazy to try and go back to sleep for an hour."

She stifled a yawn. "What time is it?"

"Just after 4:30. Go back to bed if you want to, Casey. You don't have to stay up here."

"Who could sleep?" She gave a rueful shrug. "Besides, it's been a long time since I've seen a mountain sunrise."

Keir smiled but said nothing and for a long while they traveled in compatible silence. Casey closed her eyes and listened to the soft music Keir had found on the radio. It wasn't until he had pulled off the highway and brought the van to a stop that she realized she had dozed off.

They were in a mountain turnout over-looking a wide canyon. She looked questioning at Keir. He grinned at her as he shut off the engine, his eyes dancing. "Come with me," he whispered.

He climbed out of the van, shutting his door quietly behind him, and Casey, with a puzzled look, followed. The cold hit her as she climbed out of the van, but it was soon forgotten in the stillness as Keir drew her in front of him and turned her toward the canyon.

"Your sunrise."

He couldn't have timed it better. The sky was already spreading its promise of a new day as it progressively lightened above the trees; a stark contrast to the dark, bluish-purple shadows of the canyon below. The sun, like a frightened child peering from behind its mother's apron, came peeping over the top of the ridge; a timid, dome-shaped sun that sent a hail of lighted shafts streaking across the canyon. Casey watched in awe as they ricocheted off the opposite ridge top to display an array and brightness of colors across the awakening canyon. Fields of green manzanita glowed and shone and sparkled all at once in an explosion of pure brilliance. Shafts of lighted arrows shimmered through the trees, lighting everything in their paths.

The contrast of brightness and shadow became intense while the sun haltingly struggled to attain its true stature. Then suddenly, as if breaking all restraints, the sun leaped from behind the ridge and bathed the whole canyon in its warmth and light.

Encased in Keir's arms, Casey stood mesmerized, soaking in the beauty and freshness of the new day. She had seen sunrises before, but none such as this.

"That was...something," she whispered at last. "Thank you, Keir."

"There's nothing quite like it," he said softly, drawing her closer against him. His arms tightened comfortably and Casey felt a feather light kiss on the top of her head. Sweetness spread through her, as well as a contentment she had never quite felt before.

"Casey?" Her name was just a breath. He turned her gently and without another word, bent his head and his lips met hers.

It wasn't a passionate kiss. It was more like the sunrise itself; sweet and fresh, and full of warmth and promise. Casey's arms crept up and around his neck and the kiss, as like the sunrise, burst forth suddenly, shooting warm rays of emotion throughout her senses.

Keir lifted his head and smiled down at her. "You know, you're quite something yourself, T'Casey Hammond." He smoothed the hair from her face and slowly lowered his lips to hers a second time as he drew her closer to him.

Casey felt warmth clear down to her toes. "Oh, my," she said on a gulp.

"Oh, my." Keir released a contented breath. "You definitely are something, Casey Hammond."

She flushed with a half-grin. "Blame it on the sunrise."

Warm laughter escaped Keir. "You make me almost regret we're leaving the mountains."

"Almost?"

A warm smile lit his eyes. "Believe me, the sunsets along the coast are just as awe-inspiring." He bent and placed a feather light kiss on her lips and took her hand.

"Hungry?"

Casey nodded. She was also light-headed and excited and very susceptible to his touch but she wasn't about to tell him that.

"Let's see if we can find something," he said, squeezing her hand. "I think there's a fair-sized town not too far up the road."

The town of Dover was not as big as Keir had expected, but it didn't matter much as he found them a place to eat not too far from the highway. Chenin and

Cortney were up by then and Keir ordered for them all. Casey again found herself eating much more than she was used to for breakfast. Maybe it was the mountain air, she mused.

Keir had the van serviced after breakfast and Chenin and Casey quickly rolled the sleeping bags and put the van back into general order before Keir had them back on the highway. Both Chenin and Cortney were squeezed together in the front seat this time and Casey could hear them happily conversing with Keir.

In English. Twice she had heard Keir remind them about avoiding their own language. "It's important for your safety," he had said. "Speaking in Thernian draws attention to you and at the moment, we don't want that. So speak only English. It will help you become fluent in the language and considering you're going to be living here in the United States you will need to be fluent. Besides," he had admitted with a grin, "I don't really know enough Thernian to understand you well."

Cortney and Chenin had giggled but they had promised him that they would do their best to use the English language.

Casey settled back, switching her thoughts to her own cousin. Donald would be back by now. Had he noticed her absence yet? She hoped not. He would likely be concerned by her sudden disappearance and she really did not want him to worry. She would have to phone him later and let him know she was safe and all right.

At least she was still on vacation from work. They wouldn't be expecting her in for another three days yet. Would she be back in time?

"Keir?"

He flickered a glance at her through the rear-view mirror. "What is it, Casey?"

"Have you found out anything yet about your parents; how long they might be?"

"Not as yet. I still couldn't get through to them this morning."

Casey frowned.

"Why? What is it, Casey?"

She moved up behind the seats. "It's just that I am due back to work Thursday."

"Any hope of an extension?"

"A permanent one," she said.

"I see…Would you mind terribly, Casey?"

"If it was permanent?"

He nodded.

"I suppose not," she said slowly, "but good jobs aren't too easy to find."

"No, I imagine they aren't. What do you do, Casey?"

"I'm a receptionist at the Ryerson Business Association."

Cortney looked over. "What is a receptionist?"

"A person who answers telephones, greets people when they come into our building, and answers standard mail," Casey said.

"Is it a lot of work, then?"

"It can be." She sat down on the floor just behind the two seats. "What do you do, Keir?"

"Teach," he said with a grin, keeping his eyes on the traffic.

"High school?"

"No. Sixth grade." He glanced at his cousin. "Do you read English yet, Cortney?"

"No, T'Keir. But I must learn."

Keir nodded. "We'll have to get you started then. You'll have to learn to write as well, both you and Chenin."

"I'll help," Casey volunteered.

Keir grinned at her. "I'll take you up on that. Maybe we can stop and pick up some paper and a few books later today."

"And some groceries?"

Keir nodded. "Definitely some groceries. Why don't you make out a grocery list, Casey? There should be a tablet in one of the drawers back there."

Casey found the tablet with minimum effort and sitting at the small table in the back proceeded to make up a grocery list. Knowing they had limited space in the van, she tried to make it short. Chenin joined her wanting to make sure she would include the ingredients for her pie.

"Have you decided what kind, Chenin?"

"Well, apple is *my* favorite. That would be okay, T'Casey, that we make an apple pie?"

Casey nodded.

"But, T'Casey?"

"Yes?"

Chenin looked up at her. "You would cut the apples for me? T'Keir does not want me using the knives."

Casey smiled. "I'll gladly cut the apples for you." She was also glad that Keir had set some limitations on the girl's cooking attempts!

Chenin's whole face seemed to smile. "Then we can make it today, T'Casey?"

"Let's leave it for tomorrow. We still have a long way to go yet today."

Chenin sighed heavily, staring out the window. "It is hard to have nothing to do."

"That's what these are for," Casey said holding up a deck of cards as she put the list aside. "Come on. Let's sit on the floor and I'll teach you how to play."

Chenin eagerly complied, and for the next hour, Casey taught her, and Cortney when he joined them, how to play Go Fish. By the end of the game, both children were able to recognize and identify the numbers up to ten in English, as well as the letters A,J,Q, and K.

"Not a bad start," Keir said when she slipped into the seat beside him awhile later.

Casey flushed. "They had fun." She glanced back at the two children. They had started a game of their own with the cards and looked as if they were enjoying themselves.

Keir brought her attention back to him. "So what did you put on your grocery list?"

Casey listed the grocery items she had written down. Keir added more items to the list. "I think we should also stop at a department store of some kind."

"I was hoping so." There were a few things she could use from a department store as well.

He chuckled softly.

Casey smiled wryly and stared out the window at a passing car. It was a lot like Donald's car and her thoughts went back to her cousin. "Keir?"

"Yes?"

"Would it be all right if I called my cousin?" He's likely to worry if he can't get in touch with me, especially with me having his car."

"Don't worry about your cousin's car, Casey," Keir told her. "I sent Karl after it. It should be back at your apartment by now."

"Thank you," Casey said with obvious relief. "Donald would not be very happy with me if I had let anything happen to it. He…" She stopped as a new thought crossed her mind; one that didn't bear thinking about.

"Casey? What is it?" There was concern in Keir's glance.

She looked over at him. "Do you think they would trace Donald's car? Because if they did…"

Keir reached over and squeezed her hand, keeping it in his. "They don't have any reason to think it's not your car," he said gently, "Not with Karl returning it to the front of your apartment and no registration in it."

"What did you do with the registration?"

I stuck it in your bill box back at your apartment. Your wallet I brought along. That's under your seat, Casey."

Casey flushed, thankful Keir had had the sense to bring it along. If the nadarb had found it…

She shuddered, unable to finish the thought and Keir's hand tightened around hers. "Don't worry about it, *avi*."

She bit her lip. "Do you think they'll find my apartment?"

"Most likely, considering I gave Karl your address and told him to pass it on to them if they asked."

Casey stared at him.

His eyes flickered to her and then back to the road. "For Karl's sake. If they don't think he's holding anything back they're likely to leave him alone."

"Do you think they'll go to my apartment?" she asked after a moment.

"Just to be sure we aren't still there," he said. "Chances are they're in Washington by now." He flickered another glance at her. "Go ahead and call your cousin when we stop. Just so he knows you're all right."

"Thanks. I'll do that. He'd panic if he thought something had happened to me."

"So would I," Keir muttered softly. "So would I."

Chapter TWELVE

Casey woke with a start as Keir pulled the van into the service station and brought it to a stop.

"Chenin's got to go," he said.

Casey stifled a yawn and climbed out of the van, taking Chenin with her.

"And Casey?"

She stopped and looked back at Keir.

"Go ahead and try to reach your cousin."

"Thanks, I will." Casey took Chenin to the restroom and then tried calling her cousin, with no luck, before heading back to the van. Keir looked at her questioning.

"He wasn't in. I'll have to try again later."

He nodded then glanced at the two children with her. "Hungry?" he asked them.

Both vigorously nodded their heads. Keir took them to the nearest McDonald's then stopped off at the large shopping center across the street.

"See what you can find," he said to Casey, nodding toward the department store. "I'll meet you inside in a few minutes."

He disappeared, and Casey, with nothing else to do, took the two children into the store.

"T'Casey!" Chenin cried out almost immediately. "We have forgotten our list."

"No, we didn't," Casey said pulling the list from her pocket. What she didn't have however was much money. Did Keir have enough? He hadn't come expecting to travel all over the countryside with her and two healthy, hungry children with needs other than just food.

She pulled a cart from the rack, deciding on the bare necessities first. The rest could wait until she knew how much they had available to spend. But despite her good intentions of sticking to necessities, Keir found them in the toy department.

"Good. I was hoping you would think of this."

Casey's glance left the children and went to him. "Keir, what about money? We still have to get some groceries and I haven't a lot."

"Don't worry about it, Casey," he said soothingly. "I just withdrew some from the bank, and I do have my credit cards." His glance went to the children still combing the toy shelves. "Look," he said turning back to her. "Why don't you take Chenin and get her some clothes. About three summer outfits, a sweater, and three pair of long pants. And a swimsuit. I'll do the same with Cortney. Then we can meet back here in toys in about forty-fifty minutes. And Casey, get anything you feel you need for yourself, okay?"

She flushed and nodded, taking Chenin with her as Keir disappeared with Cortney. Chenin, she found, was very easy to shop for, for she was thrilled and satisfied with anything Casey thought was appropriate. Their shopping, including underwear, socks, and a new pair of tennis shoes for them both as well as other necessities, was done in just over forty minutes. Casey headed back to the toy department with a full cart.

To her surprise, Keir's cart was even fuller. "I picked up a few extra sweat suits and a couple of light jackets," he said, catching her eye. "The beach can get rather chilly at times."

"Did you get any books?"

"I thought I'd do that while the kids were looking at toys. Stay with them, will you?" And he was off again, leaving her with the carts as well as Chenin and Cortney.

Casey watched as the two children carefully combed the toy shelves a second time.

"Can we touch them?" Cortney was watching several other children.

"If you're very careful."

Chenin, after one quick look at the other toys, glued herself in front of the dolls, not taking her eyes off one in particular. Casey knelt down beside her.

"You like her, Chenin?"

"She is beautiful, T'Casey."

Casey picked up the box. "It says her name is Amberleigh and she likes to listen to stories and songs."

"Amberleigh," Chenin whispered.

Casey opened the box and carefully removed the doll. She then pretended to read the outside of the box. "It also says that she needs a home and someone to love her. Would you like to be that someone, Chenin?"

Chenin looked from the doll, to Casey. "Do you really mean that, T'Casey? Can she really belong to me?"

"I really mean it." Casey held out the doll to her. "There's even a blanket and a nightgown for her in the box."

Chenin took the doll and hugged it to her, her eyes shining. "I love her, T'Casey!"

Casey smiled at the girl. She stood up, putting the doll's box in her cart, unsure of what Keir would say. The doll was not a cheap one. But, did it matter? The doll had Chenin's heart and she would buy it herself if need be.

"T'Casey?" Cortney was standing beside her, holding a large box of old fashioned cars. "Do you think maybe T'Keir would let me chose these?"

"T'Keir says yes," Keir said from behind them. He plopped the books and supplies he had found into his basket. He grinned at Casey. "I'd say we've got just about everything."

"You sure you don't want to throw in a kitchen sink?"

He grinned. "We've already got one." He led them to the checkouts then handed Casey several large bills. "Why don't you get started on the groceries next door? It will save us time. We'll join you as soon as we get these through and put up."

Casey complied knowing he was right. They needed to get back on the road soon if they intended to get to the Pacific Ocean at a decent time. She hurried across the parking lot and into the grocery store, wondering if she could make it through the store while Keir and the children were still checking out. They hadn't been first in line, and they themselves had two carts to check through, not to mention putting it all into the van. Besides, she did not have that much to get.

She almost made it. She was in the checkout line when they joined her. Keir took a quick, but thorough glance at the items she had collected. "Tell them we want two bags of crushed ice as well."

Casey stared at him. "Keir, we don't have room for all that!"

A grin came out of him. "We do now. I'll be right back."

Casey watched him go with exasperation. What did he do, buy a full-sized refrigerator?

"Just an ice chest," he corrected when he returned a few minutes later carrying four cases of canned soft drinks.

Just an ice chest?

"Keir Jairon! Do you have *any* money left?"

"Lots," he said with a touch of amusement.

Casey seriously doubted it when she climbed into the van several minutes later. There were bags everywhere, as well as a large box containing the ice chest. Keir added the groceries and slipped behind the wheel. "Is everyone in?"

They were once more on their way.

With a muted sigh, Casey unloaded the ice chest from its box and put the children to work separating the canned sodas and putting both them and the ice away in the ice chest. She began on the perishable groceries, loading them into the van's small refrigerator. Surprisingly it held more than she expected. She shoved half of the fruit into the leftover space and then began on the dry goods. Finished at last with the groceries, she turned and attacked the rest of the bags.

It wasn't hard really. The box the ice chest came in became a wardrobe for the children's clothes, which took care of the majority of the bags. The rest was just a matter of shoving things here or there. The jackets, three new ones, she hung up in the tiny closet, next to Keir's older, brown one.

She moved the ice chest up behind the two seats and sat down on it. "Keir, you didn't buy a jacket for me, did you?"

"Just in case you need it," he said. He glanced at the two sitting in the seat beside him. "Casey, do you think you could set up the bed back there? Chenin's out already and it looks like Cortney's almost there."

Casey stood up again. "What about you, Keir? You look like you could use some rest yourself." He'd been on the go since early morning now.

"I'm okay."

"Sure you are," she muttered lowering the table and rearranging the cushions. She's give him an hour, no longer, and then she'd boot him into the back. She helped Cortney and Chenin to the bed and then sat down beside Keir.

"Where are we?"

"Just inside the Oregon border."

"We still have a ways to go then, don't we?"

"A ways. I figure we'll get there sometime between eight and nine o'clock tonight, depending on how many times we need to stop."

Casey leaned back, watching the scenery go by. "Are these still the Rocky Mountains we're in?"

"Well, yes and no. We're still in the Rockies, though this particular range we're in is considered the Blue Mountains."

"Is Raccoon Creek in the mountains?"

"In the Smoke River Mountains, and yes, they're part of the Rockies."

"Do I dare ask which part?"

He laughed softly. "In Idaho, Casey."

"I see." She glanced over at him. "Where in Oregon is Turtle Sands?"

"Turtle Sands is midway down the Oregon coast."

"That's a long way from Seattle."

"A very long way." He shot her an amused smile, "That's why we sent them there."

"Do you think they'll give up?"

Keir smothered a yawn. "They're likely to soon, Casey. It won't take them long to realize that they were led on a wild goose chase. They'll know Chenin and Cortney most likely made it safely to my father. And once they report in…"

"Don't say it." Casey shuddered.

"At least the kids will be safe." He smothered another yawn. "Casey, do you really think you could drive this thing?"

"As long as it's an automatic shift."

"Great," he said in relief, "Because I'm beat. Just let me find a place to pull over and I'll let you drive."

He found one not too far up the road. "Just stay on the highway," he said as she slipped behind the wheel. "We're taking it all the way through Bend then take Highway 20 to Corvallis."

He stumbled back toward his young cousins, and Casey, with a satisfied grin, pulled the van back into traffic.

"T'Casey. I am thirsty."

Casey sent a startled glance in Cortney's direction. She hadn't heard him get up. "Why don't you get us each a soda out of the ice chest." She smiled at him. "I'm thirsty, too."

The boy willingly dug through the ice chest, coming up with two. He sat down in the seat beside her. "Why are we going so slow?"

"They're working on the road," Casey told him, glad of his company. She had been driving three hours straight and it was beginning to wear on her.

"Here is your soda," he said getting it opened at last.

Casey took the cold can from him and drank thirstily. "Thanks, Cortney. It's just what I needed." She smiled, feeling better. The soda had certainly helped. "Are Chenin and Keir still sleeping?"

"T'Keir is, but I think Chenin is trying to wake up. T'Casey, what is that man doing with the small flag?"

"Waving us on," she said with relief. The construction was over. Casey increased her speed, taking another drink from the cold can. "Are you hungry, Cortney?"

"Yes," he said, glancing at her.

She sent him a smile. "So am I. Go look in the cupboard under the refrigerator. You'll find a bag with some meat in it. Bring it here."

Again the boy readily complied. He held up a bag of beef jerky. "Is this it?"

"That's it. Can you get it open?"

Cortney sat down and struggled with it. "There," he said with satisfaction. "It is open. What kind of meat is this, T'Casey?"

"It's called beef jerky."

He handed her a piece, then took one for himself and for a moment they ate in silence.

"What is that you are eating?" It was Chenin, with her doll tucked under her arm.

"Beef jerky," her brother said, handing her a piece.

She turned to Casey. "We are not there yet, T'Casey?"

"I'm afraid not, Chenin," Casey said. She glanced briefly at the girl.

Chenin stood a moment, silently tasting the beef jerky. "T'Casey, I have to go to the...bathroom."

Casey shot her another look. "Can you wait a few minutes, Chenin?" She had already decided to stop in the next town to put a call through to Donald, as well as get gas.

Chenin slid into the seat beside her brother and whispered something in his ear. Cortney handed her his can of soda. She took a drink and handed it back to him then turned to Casey. "T'Casey, will you tell a story to us? Please?" She plopped her doll onto her lap. "Amberleigh would like a story."

"A story?"

The child nodded.

Casey thought a minute. "Have you heard the story about Goldilocks and the three bears?"

Chenin shook her head. She took a bite of the beef jerky and looked expectantly at Casey.

"Well," Casey began, "way back, a long, long time ago, in the deep woods, there lived a family of three bears…"

Both children listened with rapt attention as Casey unfolded the story. Not even the stop at the service station interrupted their interest.

"Tell us another one," they both begged when she had finished. Casey began the story of the three Billy Goats Gruff.

"Oh, this one I know!" Chenin cried out in delight.

"You sure you want me to tell it to you, then?"

"Oh, yes, T'Casey!"

Casey was finishing her fourth fairy tale when Keir finally joined them.

"You can come and tell stories to my class anytime," he said removing a soda from the ice chest before sitting down on it. A yawn came out of him. "Where are we?"

"On Highway 20 heading for Corvallis," she told him.

"Good grief. You should have woke me, Casey."

Casey bristled. "Why?"

Keir studied her a moment then shook his head and turned to his young cousins. "How are you two doing?"

"We are doing fine, T'Keir," Cortney answered for them both. "T'Casey has been telling stories to us."

"So I've heard. Are any of you hungry?"

"I am," both children said together.

"I bet you are." Keir grinned as he noted the empty jerky bag. "Casey?"

"A little…What time is it?"

"Almost five."

"Already?" Casey could not believe she had driven all afternoon. Where had the time gone?

"Casey, if you're all right, I'll go ahead and make sandwiches for all of us. Then, when you get tired..."

Casey nodded. "Could you get me another soda first?"

He opened the ice chest. "Anything special?"

"Root beer?"

"Sure." He opened a can and handed it to her. "Just let me know if you want to stop, will you?"

"Will do." Casey sent him a mock salute.

Keir turned and began rummaging through the cupboards with Chenin and Cortney's help, and Casey turned her concentration back to her driving.

"T'Casey, will you teach us to play cards again, please?" Dinner had been over hours ago and Keir was again behind the wheel.

"Sure, Chenin," Casey said, trying to muster some enthusiasm. It was hard. She was tired of traveling. They all were.

"T'Casey, may I have something more to eat?"

Her head shook. "No, Cortney. I think you had better wait until morning. It's almost bedtime."

The boy sat dejectedly beside his sister, his hands traveling to the medallion around his neck and around it. He was still searching for his life-ring.

"Come on, Cortney," Casey said trying to sound cheerful. "You deal first this time."

The card game was only a temporary diversion Casey noted later as she handed the sleeping bags to Cortney, for he was again looking lost and depressed. She helped settle them both into their bags then slipped into the seat beside Keir. He looked all in.

"Tired?"

"Yes." He shot her a glance. "You look beat."

"I guess we all are." Her voice softened. "Keir, what are we going to do about Cortney's ring? He's still missing it dreadfully."

Keir gave a heavy sigh. "I don't know, Casey. I don't think there's much we can do."

"Can't we replace it, and pretend we found it?"

Keir slipped the silver chain carrying his own life-ring over his head and handed it to Casey. "Look inside."

Casey did as she was instructed, surprised to find Keir's name and birthdate engraved on the inside of the tiny ring. She looked at him in amazement. "But it's so small!"

"Big enough." He grinned then sobered immediately. "Cortney's name should be engraved in his as well."

"I see." Casey absently studied the ring in her hands. "Is it silver?"

"White gold."

"White gold? I've never heard of it." Casey continued to study the ring.

Keir shrugged. "It's a gold alloy. Gold is generally too soft to retain a shape of its own, so it's usually combined with another metal, in this case, silver."

"Is Cortney's white gold, then?"

"Most likely….Do you have a baby ring, Casey?"

"Somewhere." Casey handed him back the life-ring.

"You don't know where it is?"

She shrugged. "The bottom of my hope chest, I think. I haven't thought about it for ages." She watched as he slipped the chain back over his head. "Keir, couldn't we get Cortney another ring anyway?"

"It wouldn't be the same thing, Casey."

"Not even if it was a symbol of his new life that's beginning here in America?"

Keir was silent a moment. "You might have something there," he said slowly. "Let me talk to my father about it."

Casey sighed and turned her eyes to the darkening sunset. It would be gone soon, and then they would be driving in darkness. "How much further?"

"About an hour and a half. Why don't you go back with the kids?"

Casey shook her head. "No, I'm okay, unless you're trying to be rid of me for a while?"

"Never," he said, shooting her a smile. "Who else would I get to hand me my drinks?"

"Chauvinist," she retorted. "Or are you hinting for a soda?"

"I wouldn't mind one," he said. "And some beef jerky, if there's any left."

Casey found him both then settled back with a soda of her own. "Keir, are you going to allow Chenin and Cortney to keep putting the 'T' in front of our names?"

He sighed tiredly. "I've been meaning to talk to them about it."

"It might be difficult for them." Though the two children had switched to English fairly well in all other areas, they hadn't given up the 'T' when addressing them.

Keir's head nodded. "Too true. I'll talk to them regardless."

"Maybe you can allow them to use it when we're alone."

His head shook. "It will be easier for them in the long run if they simply drop it from all speech. That way they aren't likely to slip up at the wrong time." He was quiet a moment. "Casey?"

She looked at him.

"Have you notified your job that you most likely won't be back?"

She flushed. "No. Considering your parents could be there by the time we arrive, or within the next day or two, I thought I would wait."

He nodded.

There was quiet for a moment. "What kind of books do you like to read?" she asked him determined to keep him talking and awake.

A grin came out of him. "All books."

"What are some of your favorites?"

Keir willingly accepted the topic and for a while they talked about the books they liked, then moved on to movies and songs and other things as they continued to drive.

Chapter THIRTEEN

Casey woke to the strong scent of sea air and the thunderous pounding of the surf. She could hear the seagulls' piercing cries as they circled the beach, and in the far off distance, the bark of sea lions.

Turtle Sands.

A thrill of excitement ran through Casey. She glanced at Keir asleep in the bag beside hers, and for a moment her glance lingered. It had been late when they had pulled into the campground, and not wanting to disturb the two sleeping children, Keir had set up her sleeping bag beside his in the front of the van. And she had not objected, not that there had been any reason to object, she told herself ignoring the pleasure it had created having him close. After all, he had only given her *one* good-night kiss. Just one. And it hadn't even been a passionate kiss, just a gentle meeting of their lips before he had rolled over and gone to sleep.

But his lips had momentarily lingered and her toes had warmed, and she had slept in blissful contentment.

Smiling, she pulled her eyes from him and after a quick look at his two sleeping cousins, she slid quietly from her sleeping bag and dressed.

Another thrill ran through her as she slipped outside. Her eyes fastened themselves immediately on the beach and the waves that thundered themselves against it unceasingly, one after another.

It was everything her cousin had told her it would be; exciting and exhilarating and slightly overwhelming. The air was cold and wet and breezy though Casey hardly noticed as she headed across the sand to the water's edge.

The waves captured her. Swelling and curling and crashing around, over, and against one another, racing to the beach where they hurriedly rolled across the sand then ran back into the ocean to do it all again. There was no continuity to the waves. Some broke and curled from one end, some from the other, and still others from the middle outwards. Like electricity, these curls rushed down the lengths of their waves in an upsurge of watery spray pounding into the surf and onto the sandy beach. It was never-ending. Thunder and rushing water echoed unceasingly through Casey, touching some deep inner cord within her.

She turned and began to make her way along the edge of the wet sand. Like a child, she let the water play tag with her feet as it ran across the sand and ebbed back, only to come running across the sand once again.

Her eyes were everywhere as she walked on, finding shells and seaweed, tiny crabs and smooth stones as the waves brought them briefly on the shore before washing them back into the sea. She didn't try to pick them up, they were on display too briefly for that, but contented herself instead with catching sight of them and everything else she could see; the mist that hovered between sea and shore, the sea gulls that flew overhead and squabbled on the beach, even the ducks feeding among the waves further out.

Everything excited and amazed her. The sights, the sounds, the feel of the sea as it rose up to meet the shore. Yet at the same time it all brought an odd sense of peace.

Realizing she had been out for a good half-hour, she turned and headed back toward the campground, walking slowly as she continued to look at everything. Two seagulls caught her attention as they squabbled on the wet sand over some sort of shell they had found and Casey stopped to watch them, a slight grin on her face. A third seagull joined the first two and without wasting a moment it reached in and grabbed the object of contention and flew away with it.

Casey laughed...until the wave she hadn't been watching came charging over the wet sand and hit her squarely, plunging her shoes and half her jeans in cold ocean water as it spread out over the shore. Almost before she could move the wave receded, its backwash eating the sand away beneath her feet causing her to almost lose her balance.

She righted herself and moved quickly to safer sand then looked down. Her jeans and shoes were soaked. Great. And that ocean water was cold! Even colder with the cool breeze blowing.

Shaking the water off her legs and shoes, she began jogging. Her thoughts went to Keir's parents as she headed back up the beach. Had they arrived? She hoped and prayed so for Chenin and Cortney's sake. They would be safe at last.

She began to wonder what his parents were like, wonder if they would really be willing to take in the children. After all, they had to be somewhere in their fifties, considering Keir was already in his late twenties, and Chenin and Cortney were still so young. Would they be as kind and caring and understanding as Keir was? Karl Banning had implied they were wonderful people, that they would be more than willing to take the children in. She sent a prayer up to the Good Lord that it would be so.

The campground came into view and Casey slowed to a walk as she found her way to the van. To her surprise Keir was gone. Chenin and Cortney were inside, looking out the back of the van window.

"Cortney, out," Casey said immediately.

The boy stared at her. "But T'Keir said…"

Casey shivered. "Please, Cortney. I've got to change."

The boy, with one last look at her, did as he was told. Casey locked the door and stripped off her wet shoes and jeans as she hunted for something warm to wear. She settled on one of the new sweat suits Keir had purchased.

"You can let Cortney back in," she said as she pulled on a pair of socks and began lacing her new shoes.

Cortney came back into the van immediately followed by Keir. The boy joined his sister by the window again, but Keir stood and looked at Casey, taking in the pile of wet clothes on the floor. His eyes came back up to hers.

She sent him a wry smile. "I got attacked by a wave."

"I see." His eyes lit briefly with amusement. He frowned suddenly. "You're cold again, Casey. You're shivering."

"I know. Wet clothes and a cold breeze do not go together well."

He slipped off his jacket and tossed it at her. "Want me to start a fire outside or get you some hot tea?"

"I'd love some hot tea," Casey said, slipping into his warm jacket. "But the fire's not necessary. I'll be fine as soon as I warm up, so stop worrying."

"You'd better be." He poured her a cup of tea that had been warming and brought it over to her. He poured another for himself and sat down beside her.

Chenin turned and looked at her. "Did the waves scare you, T'Casey?"

Casey shook her head. "They just surprised me, Chenin. Are you afraid of the beach?" she asked, remembering the waterfall.

The girl looked surprised. "No, T'Casey. I have gone to the beach many times. "T'Keir..."

"Keir," her cousin corrected swiftly. "You must not forget what I said, Chenin."

Casey glanced at Keir. So he had remembered to discuss the use of the titled 'T' with them.

Chenin sighed dejectedly looking up at him. "I am sorry, Keir. It is just not too easy to remember."

"I know," Keir said gently. "It will just take practice, Chenin. Casey and I will help you."

"Keir?"

His eyes came back to Casey.

"Did your parents make it here?"

Keir shook his head. "I'm going to attempt to get in touch with them later. Don't worry, Casey. They'll get here."

"Just so they get here before..." She stopped abruptly not wanting to go on in front of the children.

"They will, Casey." Keir flickered a glance out the window and then over at his young cousin. "How would you like a language lesson, Cortney?"

The boy turned eagerly to Keir. "You will teach me to read English now?"

"We'll give it a good start."

"Me, also?" Chenin begged.

"You, also, *if* we can talk Casey into making us breakfast?"

Casey willingly complied. She took her time, fixing them a large breakfast as she soaked up the warmth from the small stove. Its heat spread quickly through the small camper van and it wasn't long before she discarded Keir's jacket for the lighter warmth of her sweatshirt.

"Breakfast is ready," she eventually told them, forcing them to clear the table. Cortney however, did not want to stop for breakfast. Eager to learn everything there was for him to learn he ignored his stomach and pressed his cousin to keep going. But Keir was determined to take it slow.

"Clear the table. We'll have another lesson after lunch."

"It cannot be after breakfast?"

"After lunch," Keir said again. "Casey and I have a few phone calls to make after breakfast."

"I've already called Donald," Casey said as she began setting the table. "I managed to get him yesterday."

"Oh?" Keir's eyes had locked onto her.

Casey flushed. "I just told him that I had decided to take a short traveling vacation after all."

Keir's eyes followed her as she turned back to the stove. "Nothing more?"

Casey shrugged. "I didn't see much reason in worrying him." She put the rest of the breakfast onto the table and slipped into the seat beside Chenin. She smiled determinedly at the three of them. "Now," she said holding out her hands. "Who's saying grace?"

They took their time over breakfast. Casey, with Chenin helping, cleaned up when they were finished. She then took the two children to the beach while Keir headed for the lodge in hopes of contacting his parents. Though Keir had assured her more than once that they were safe at the seaside campground, Casey stayed vigilant in keeping her eyes on the children as well as the surrounding area.

"We can get wet?" the two wanted to know immediately.

Casey shook her head. "Not this early." Though she blamed it on the still cool breeze, she didn't want to admit that she was just too nervous to let them into the ocean without Keir present. "I think we need to wait until it warms up a bit first."

The two looked undaunted. "Can we look on the sand for the shells, then?"

Casey smiled as she sat down in the dry sand. "As long as you stay where I can see you. I'll be right here."

Cortney and Chenin dashed happily enough to the water's edge and Casey contented herself with watching them. Keir joined her awhile later.

"Were you able to get in touch with your parents?"

His head shook as he settled himself down beside her. "They're likely in transit."

"So they could be here sometime today?"

"It's possible." His eyes went out to the children then back to her. "I was able to get in touch Karl. Bruen did apparently pay him a visit."

Casey's stomach jumped. "Is he okay?"

"He's fine, Casey. Bruen sort of *asked* him to tell them what he knew about you then asked about my father's address." A grin seemed to touch his face. "As he put it, he grudgingly but willingly gave them what they wanted and they left."

Relief swept through Casey. "I'm glad he's okay."

"So am I." His eyes again went to his two cousins. "They seem to be enjoying themselves."

Casey nodded. Her eyes fastened on the surf and the waves that were thundering unceasingly. "It's really something, isn't it?"

"An equal to the majestic mountains," he said in agreement, his eyes, too, on the coastline.

"Yet so vastly different."

"Yes. I suppose that's why some prefer one and some the other."

Casey pulled her eyes from the beach and eyed him curiously. "Which do you prefer?"

Keir's eyes remained on the breaking waves. "That's a hard one to answer, Casey," he said. "They are so different...so wondrous in their own ways. Of course," he added his face brightening with a warm, teasing glance, "I'm rather partial to mountain sunrises at the moment."

Casey flushed at the remembrance, not daring to mention the reference he had made to coastal sunsets. She buried her feet deeper into the sands as her eyes sought out Chenin and Cortney still playing along the water line.

She glanced again at Keir. "Do you come to the coast often?"

"Rarely...which I suppose tends to say a lot, I imagine. What about you, Casey? Do you have a preference?"

Casey brought her knees up and wound her arms around them. "I suppose it's something I'll have to discover," she said. She shot him a wry glance. "This is my first visit to the coast."

Keir stared at her in surprise. "And you lived in California most of your life?"

"Terribly neglected, wasn't I?" She grinned at his disbelief. "Would you believe I've never been to San Francisco either?"

Keir shook his head. "Some Californian."

"Ex-Californian, besides, we spent most vacations visiting relatives in Chicago, which didn't give us much time for thinking about beaches."

"Well, Miss T'Casey Hammond," Keir said as he stood and brushed the sand off his Levis, "I think it's about time you were properly introduced to the wonders of the sea."

He took her hand, gathered up his two young cousins, and together they headed along the sandy coastline. Chenin and Cortney skipped along, running ahead, playing with the waves and eager to point out the wondrous sights and sounds that caught their attention.

It was a more informative look at the sea than her earlier walk. Casey, like the children, did not hesitate to ask Keir the multitude of questions that surfaced as she walked along, and Keir, with the patience born in an outstanding teacher, did his best to answer them in a way that his young cousins could understand.

It was well after noon when they finally returned to the van. Casey fed them a light lunch then Keir took the time to give his cousins another lesson in reading. Casey gave them an hour before ushering both Keir and Cortney outside so that Chenin could begin on her apple pie.

It was only then that Casey realized how well the child could cook. Though Casey cut the apples for her, Chenin needed very little of Casey's help after that as she made the apple filling from scratch, not that there was much to it Casey admitted, just four added ingredients, but she was impressed regardless for the girl had accomplished it without any recipe. That was something Casey knew she had never done. She helped Chenin pour it into the pre-prepared pie crust they had bought earlier and slip it into the oven. The pie came out wonderful.

"She's going to give me a complex," Casey said to Keir as they sat eating it that night. "I doubt if I've ever made a pie from scratch."

Keir grinned lazily. "I guess you're going to have to start taking lessons from her, aren't you?"

"Thanks," Casey retorted sourly. She stood up and began gathering the dirty dishes. Did Keir really believe she needed lessons in cooking?

"Casey."

She turned to find him behind her.

"There's nothing wrong with your culinary skills, believe me. Your cooking is wonderful. Which reminds me," he said with a teasing light, "I haven't yet thanked you for dinner, have I?"

"Keir--"

"Hush, *sher'avi*," he whispered as his lips descended to hers.

The warm kiss lingered long after he disappeared down the path toward the lodge. Casey stood bemused. For someone whose heart belonged elsewhere, Keir Jairon did a generous amount of kissing.

Was it possible that his heart wasn't as attached as he thought?

The thought resurfaced a while later when he walked them down to the beach and they sat in the warm, dry sand and watched the sun set.

"That was beautiful, Keir," she said contentedly as the colors disappeared with the sun and the light of the sky began fading into night.

"That it was," he agreed. He pulled her gently to her feet and his arms came around her. "Just as beautiful as this will be," he said and tilting her chin, took her lips in a warm, gentle kiss.

Chapter FOURTEEN

As one day turned into the next Casey's worry over Keir's parents grew. They still hadn't arrived and despite Keir's efforts, he did not seem to be able to get in touch with them. Wednesday afternoon she called into work explaining that she wouldn't be making it back, not at least for another three or four days.

"I'll give you until Monday," her boss told her. "Otherwise I'll have no choice but to let you go."

Casey thanked him for his understanding and hung up.

Thursday morning Keir finally received word from his parents in the form of a telegram:

PROBLEMS ON THIS END. NOW STRAIGHTENED. WILL BE THERE SATURDAY. KEEP CHILDREN SAFE.

Relief filled Casey that Keir had finally heard from them yet she worried that they wouldn't be arriving until Saturday. "I wonder what kind of problems they had?"

"Who knows, Casey? At least they're finally in touch." Even Keir sounded relieved.

The rest of Thursday morning was spent teaching Chenin and Cortney the fine art of reading and writing

English and the afternoon was spent down on the beach. That night they again sat and watched the sun set.

Thursday drifted into Friday.

Misty sunshine greeted Casey as she woke Friday morning. She lay for a moment, listening to the sounds of the surf. Would she ever get used to it? It had been three days already and it stilled thrilled her. Three days of beach combing, swimming, picnics, and studying.

And worrying about Keir's parents, she admitted. But at least that worry had eased. They would be here tomorrow. And then Chenin and Cortney would be safe and secure at last.

Not that they hadn't been safe. As Keir had said, the campground was far enough away from Washington not to be considered and obscure enough off the main paths to be passed by. Yet despite his assurances, Casey had still worried though the worry had grown less and less.

Because of Keir? Casey flushed. She liked Keir. She liked everything about him; his softly accented voice, his grin and his warm, smiling eyes. She liked his humor, his intelligence, and his strength. And, she admitted, she liked his arms around her. Her thoughts drifted to the evening walks they had taken through the ocean sunsets. They had held hands, and kissed, and sometimes she had just sat and watched the sunset encased in Keir's arms. If it hadn't been for the children...

If it hadn't been for the children, she wouldn't even be here, she reminded herself wryly. She slipped quietly out of her sleeping bag and dressed. Chenin and Cortney were still sleeping deeply, and Keir, she noted, was already up and gone. She grabbed the jacket that had been purchased for her and slipped outside.

"Good morning, *avi*," Keir greeted her almost immediately. "Would you like some coffee?"

"Coffee?" she said in hopeful surprise.

"Coffee." Keir grinned as he handed her a cup. "I hope you don't mind?"

Casey shook her head, sipping the hot liquid. "It's great. Thanks, Keir. I was beginning to think tea was all the Jairons drank."

A warm chuckle came out of him as he poured himself another cup. "Not quite. Even Mom likes a change once in a while. Do you prefer coffee?"

She shrugged. "Usually in the mornings."

"You should have said something, Casey."

She shrugged again and finding a log close to the fire, sat down. "Your tea was just as good...How long have you been up?"

"An hour or so," he said throwing a few more pieces of driftwood into the flames. "You sleep well?"

"Wonderfully."

He glanced at her. "I talked to my father this morning. They're flying into New York sometime today then taking the first flight they can find to Oregon."

Relief filled Casey. "Thank goodness. What was their hang-up?"

"You really want to know?"

Casey nodded.

"Okay. First off, the message I left him when I called from your apartment got somehow waylaid when the convention was moved to France for one reason or another. It apparently didn't catch up with him until Monday evening."

"Monday! Oh, my."

"That isn't the half of it," Keir told her shaking his head. "The first flight they tried to book they missed due to the bus taking them to the airport breaking down. The second flight was cancelled. Their third wasn't a direct flight. It flew them to England, then on to Holland. At the moment they're in Amsterdam waiting for the connection to New York, which should be leaving sometime soon."

"No wonder you haven't been able to reach them."

Keir nodded. "Dad finally got through to the campground here about thirty minutes ago to let me know what was going on. He said they'd call again when their flight reaches Oregon which most likely will be tomorrow morning; not that he knows where in Oregon they'll be landing."

Casey shook her head. "At least we now know they're on their way."

"Definitely a relief. Now we can actually relax for the day." Keir shifted positions. "Casey, speaking of relaxing…"

She looked up at him.

"Would you mind terribly if I took Cortney out ocean fishing today?"

"Ocean fishing?"

"Andy Bryant, the manager here, has a boat and he's offered to take Cortney and me out. Apparently one of the couples that were going out with him today had to cancel."

"And you jumped at the chance."

Keir gave a wry shrug. "Well, considering we've heard from Dad I though it couldn't hurt…And you do have to admit, it's not something one gets the opportunity to do often. Besides, I think Cortney would really enjoy it."

"I'm sure he would," Casey said with a trace of laughter. Keir wanted to go just as much as the boy would! Her head shook. "I don't mind you going, Keir. Chenin and I will be fine. In fact, it works out for the best. We girls had plans to clean the van today."

"I see."

"How long do you think you'll be gone?"

Keir shrugged. "I really can't say, Casey. There's another couple coming as well, so I imagine it will depend on the general consensus. Does that bother you, that we could be gone all day?" He sounded genuinely concerned.

Casey shook her head to hide her disappointment. "No, not as long as you take care of yourselves. When are you supposed to be leaving?"

"Rather soon. Which means," he said as he stood and stretched, "I had better get Cortney up and going."

"Do you want breakfast before you go?"

"He'll have something ready for us on the boat." Keir handed her his empty cup. He reached out and gently touched her cheek then bent and let his lips touch hers. "Thank you, *sher'avi*," he whispered. He turned and disappeared into the van to wake his young cousin.

Cortney appeared thrilled. He dressed hurriedly and was ready to go almost before Keir. "Casey and Chenin are not coming with us?"

"Not this time," Casey said. "This trip is just for you and Keir. Just be careful, Cortney... listen to Keir and have fun."

"He will," Keir said from behind her. "I promise. You just promise to be careful yourself, and don't work too hard."

"I won't. Enjoy yourself, Keir."

"Oh, I will," he said surprising her with a warm, lingering kiss before disappearing down toward the small lodge with Cortney.

Casey, with a heavy sigh helped herself to another cup of coffee and settled back down by the fire. It seemed colder now, and lonely. She was missing him already. She gave herself a shake and forced her mind away from Keir to the day ahead while she waited for Chenin. It was almost an hour longer before the girl woke.

"Keir and Cortney, they are gone?"

"They went fishing out on that boat, way over there," Casey said pointing toward one of the boats that was slowly moving off in the distance, not that she was sure it was the right boat.

It didn't matter to Chenin. She plopped herself down on the log beside Casey. "I'm hungry, T'Casey."

"So am I." Casey sent a smile at her. "Want to keep me company while I fix some breakfast?"

"I would like that. I can help, too?"

"You can help, too." She enjoyed having Chenin to herself. They made a simple breakfast of scrambled eggs and toast, and then turned energetically to the cleaning of the van by Chenin's insistence.

"We are to clean everything, are we not?" the child asked as she began rolling up her sleeping bag.

"Everything," Casey said as she took her own sleeping bag and piled it on top of Cortney's. She reached over and took Chenin's. "Let's leave the sleeping bags until it warms up a bit. Then we can open them up and aire them outside."

Chenin readily complied, plopping Keir's bag on top of the others. She turned to her and Cortney's clothes box. "I will begin cleaning out our box, T' – I mean Casey. Is that okay?" Already she was pulling her things out.

"Definitely," Casey said. She was proud of Chenin for correcting herself. She turned and straightened her own small cupboard, then Keir's. For a while they worked in a comfortable silence as they went through the van, cleaning the cupboards and drawers, the cab, and eventually the kitchen area. But it wasn't long before Chenin begged for a story and Casey found herself going from one story to another as they worked. It was awhile before they thought of anything else.

"Casey, I am hungry."

"I wonder why," Casey said wryly as she glanced at her watch. It was already past noon. "I'll tell you what, Chenin. Just let me finish the closet here and we'll have lunch."

"I will help you fix it."

"Good enough." Casey replaced the jackets into the small closet and shut its door. "Sandwiches, okay?"

"Can it be tuna sandwiches?"

Casey nodded. "Tuna it is. Why don't you get us something to drink while I make the sandwiches?"

The girl eagerly complied. They took their lunch outside and sat at the small picnic table the campground provided. It was surprisingly warm, Casey noted, despite the slight ocean breeze. They would be able to swim today if Keir and Cortney returned in time.

She sighed unconsciously as she glanced out at the boats off in the distance, wondering which one the two were on. Had they caught anything? She hoped not. She had no idea how to prepare fresh fish; cook them, yes, but not prepare them for cooking. It was something her brother and cousin had always attended to. You had to scale them first, didn't you? And somehow remove the innards? She shuddered. No. This was one time she definitely hoped for failure.

Casey turned her attention back to Chenin as she began picking up the paper plates. "How would you like to take a walk along the beach?"

Chenin's eyes lit up. "I can collect shells?"

"You can collect shells." Though what the girl would do with any more shells, Casey didn't know. Already both children had collected a fair share of them.

Chenin shoved the last of her sandwich into her mouth and picked up her plate, helping Casey to clean up the remains of their lunch. She stopped suddenly.

"Casey. We did not yet do the sleeping bags."

"They can wait until we get back." Casey held out her hand to Chenin. "Come on. Let's go have some fun."

Chapter FIFTEEN

The breeze was slightly cooler nearer the beach, due no doubt, to the mists that were still rising from the crashing waves, hovering wetly between sea and shore, yet the air was still warm. The beach was dotted with people now. Kids were dashing back and forth as they played with the waves. Parents were sitting under beach umbrellas watching them. The water looked inviting.

"We can go swimming, Casey?"

"Maybe later, if Keir agrees," Casey said. She still was not used to swimming in the ocean, and felt uneasy taking Chenin in without Keir around.

"He will be back soon, with Cortney?"

"I don't know," Casey said lightly. "We'll just have to hope so."

"I miss Cortney and Keir being with us."

"So do I, Chenin." And not just for his companionship, she admitted glancing around again. She felt safer when Keir was with them.

Chenin let go of Casey's hand and dashed across the wet sand to the water's edge. "Look, Casey!" Pride resounded in her voice as she held up a perfect shell.

But Casey wasn't looking at the shell. "Chenin!"

The warning was too late as Chenin was knocked off her feet and swept up the sand by an incoming wave. Casey was beside her in a flash, pulling her to her feet.

A giggle came out of Chenin. "I am all right, Casey. Look, I even saved...Casey, look out!"

It was another incoming wave. They scurried to the safety of drier sand, barely avoiding the second wave. Casey looked down at Chenin. She was dripping wet, but grinning, the shell still gripped triumphantly in her hand.

"You will keep this for me, Casey?" She was holding up the shell.

Casey absently took the shell from her. "Don't you want to go change?"

The girl stopped, suddenly deflated. "Yes, Casey."

"Hey, you don't have to," Casey said. It wasn't cold enough to hurt the child.

Chenin brightened. "I really do not need to, Casey. The sun will dry me. Truly."

Casey laughed. "I believe it will, Chenin."

Chenin gave Casey an impulsive hug and dashed off again, hunting newer shells. She wasn't particular about her choices. She picked up anything that caught her eye and gave it to Casey for safe keeping. She stopped only when she realized Casey could carry no more.

"Do you think my cousin Keir will allow me to keep these shells, too?"

"I'm sure he will," Casey said. "What are you going to do with them all?"

"I am saving them for Father," the girl said with a skip. "He likes shells." She stopped and looked up at

Casey, a pensive look on her face. "Will it be long yet, Casey, before Father comes to us?"

Casey's heart lurched. What could she say? She and Keir had told them little about their father.

"Oh, Chenin," she said going down to the girl's level, "I really can't say how long it will be. I really don't know."

The child's teeth sank into her lower lip. "It could be a long while yet, yes?"

Casey nodded. "I'm afraid so." A long, long while. Casey sent her a forced smile. "But that doesn't mean we can't get these shells ready for him. Come on. Let's go see if we can find a box to put them in."

Chenin brightened. "There were boxes behind the lodge building when Keir took me around."

There were still boxes behind the lodge when Chenin and Casey arrived. They chose one just slightly larger than a shoe box and went back to the van where Casey left Chenin washing the shells as she went in to take care of the sleeping bags before it was too late. She wanted them done before Keir returned with Cortney.

And they definitely needed airing out, she mused, finding three socks and a new hair ribbon at the bottom of Chenin's. She took it outside, gave it a good shake, and hung it across the line that the campground had provided each campsite, then headed back inside for the others.

She found a sock in hers, nothing in Keir's, and everything in Cortney's; everything from candy wrappers to underwear.

"Great." She groaned as she pulled them out. Yet, she had to admit, she was glad. At least Cortney was showing signs of being a normal boy. Adult behavior in one so young was just not normal.

Casey unzipped the rest of the bag, picked out two more socks, and picked it up. Almost immediately, another small object tumbled out and rolled under her feet…a tiny object that sparkled briefly in the sunlight before it disappeared out of sight.

Casey dropped the sleeping bag and fell to the floor of the van, not daring to acknowledge the hope that began spreading through her.

Hope that became reality, for there it was, under the edge of the small counter.

Cortney's ring.

Casey stared at it in disbelief. It had been here, in his sleeping bag all this time. The chain hadn't broken while he had played by the river, but while he slept.

The chain.

Casey scrambled back to her feet and grabbed Cortney's sleeping bag. Sure enough, the chain lay imbedded in the lining near the end of the zipper. She carefully pulled it free and sat down, staring at the chain and ring resting in her hand. She picked up the ring and looked inside it just to be sure. Cortney's name and birthdate were etched inside.

"Chenin!"

The girl's head popped in through the open doorway. "Yes, Casey?"

"Come here," Casey said, a large grin beginning to split across her face.

Chenin, a look of puzzlement on her face, did as she was told.

"Look," Casey whispered, opening her hand.

Chenin stared at the tiny, white-gold ring in Casey's hand. She swallowed. "Cortney's ring?"

Casey nodded.

"Oh, T'Casey! You have found it! You really and truly have found Cortney's ring!" She was dancing up and down.

"I know." Casey grinned at her, closing her fist once again. She pulled Chenin to her and hugged her exuberantly.

"Oh, Casey, Cortney will be so...so happy!"

"I should hope so." It would be wonderful to see the boy truly happy for once; his life-ring restored. Casey opened her fist and studied it absently. Like Keir's, it was white-gold, with a small intricate design etched around it.

Chenin, too, looked at it. "It is beautiful, is it not?"

"Yes, it is," Casey said softly.

"I, too, have a beautiful life-ring. It is like Cortney's, except for my name." She looked up. "What is your life-ring like?"

"I'm afraid I don't have one, Chenin, but I do have something similar. We call it a baby ring. My grandmother gave it to me when I was born."

"But you do not wear it?"

"I'm afraid not," Casey said. "Do you wear yours always, Chenin?"

"Always, until the day I marry." She sat down on the cushions beside Casey. "You do not exchange rings in marriage here in America?"

"We exchange wedding rings," Casey said smiling at the girl's serious face.

"But not your…baby rings?"

She shook her head.

Chenin looked up. "It is different in Thern. It is beautiful."

Casey sent Chenin another smile. "Tell me about it."

Chenin seemed eager to comply. "In Thern, a man offers his heart and his whole life by the giving of his life-ring. If the woman of his heart accepts marriage to him, she wears it beside her own."

"She doesn't give him her life-ring in return?"

"Oh, yes," Chenin said, "On the day of their marriage she gives him her life-ring, pledging her life and her heart into his care. It is then that he places the wedding band on her finger and they are man and wife. It is truly beautiful, Casey."

"It sounds beautiful," Casey replied.

"What sounds beautiful?" Keir was suddenly standing in the open doorway of the van.

"The exchanging of life-rings," Chenin said. The child jumped up, pulling him into the van. "You must show it to him, Casey!" She was again dancing up and down with excitement.

Keir raised a questioning eyebrow up in Casey's direction. She held out her hand and opened it. Cortney's ring and chain shimmered as the sun from the window hit it. Keir stared at it. "Casey? You've found Cortney's life-ring?" And when she nodded. "You've actually found it?"

Casey nodded again, unable to hide the wide grin that split across her face. "It was in the sleeping bag he's been using. The chain was lodged in the material. The ring rolled out when I picked it up."

"Oh, you beautiful, wonderful, fantastic woman!" He pulled her to him and gave her a quick, heart-rending kiss that melted her bones, and disappeared out of the van. He was back a moment later with Cortney.

"Show it to him, Casey."

Again Casey opened her hand, revealing the ring and chain.

Cortney stared at it for a long moment. He swallowed and his eyes met Casey's. "My ring? You have found it, T'Casey?"

Casey smiled gently. "Yes, Cortney. I've found it." She placed the ring and its chain into his small hand. "You'll have to have Keir fix the chain."

The boy's eyes went back to the ring. His fist abruptly closed around it and he threw himself into Casey's arms. "Oh, T'Casey! I love you! Thank you, thank you, thank you!"

Casey's heart turned over. "You're more than welcome, Cortney. You just make sure you have Keir secure the chain," she said again.

The boy nodded, releasing Casey from his hold. "T'Casey?"

Casey looked down at his serious face.

A breath expelled from him. "Thank you."

Casey smiled. "My pleasure, Cortney."

He threw himself back into her arms. "I love you," he said again.

Keir shifted. "Hey, come on you two. You're supposed to share the celebration."

"What kind of celebration are we sharing?" Chenin wanted to know.

"A wonderful one," Keir said. His warm eyes met Casey's and she felt herself melting. Never had she ever imagined that she could feel so kissed just by a glance!

She flushed and Keir's grin widened ever-so-slightly. "The lodge is holding an old fashioned clambake tonight," he said. "It would be a great way to celebrate."

Cortney looked up. "What is a clambake?"

Keir grinned. "It's a party on the beach."

Cortney grinned widely. "I like parties!"

"But we have never been to a clambake party," Chenin said. "Will we like that, too?"

Keir's grin was as wide as Cortney's. "Oh, yes, you will definitely like this, too!"

Chapter SIXTEEN

The clambake was like nothing Casey had ever experienced before. Campfires lit the beach. Music blared and guitars sang soft melodies. Food was everywhere, especially the clams that had been dug and collected by one and all. Frisbees, beach balls, volleyballs, and even horseshoes were tossed back and forth across the sand while others scrambled for more clams.

Full from eating fish, as well as the salads and other foods that had been brought, Casey sat back beside Keir, watching the two children romp in the wet sand as they attempted to throw a Frisbee back and forth. Both were in high spirits; had been since Keir had restored Cortney's chain and replaced his life-ring back around his neck.

"I'm glad we found his ring," she said, her eyes resting on an exuberant Cortney.

"So am I, *avi*," Keir murmured, his eyes too, on the boy. "It means the world to him." He shot her a quick grin. "It's been quite a day."

"Yes, it has." Not only had they found and restored Cortney's ring, but Keir and Cortney had caught more than one ocean fish while they had been out. "Thanks for donating the fish tonight," she told him, glad she hadn't had to worry about cooking them.

Keir merely grinned. "They were good, weren't they?"

"Better than the clams." It had taken only one bite for her to realize she had no liking for the shellfish.

"Didn't like the clams, huh?"

A flush rose. "I enjoyed digging for them."

"But not eating them?"

Casey's head shook. She absently adjusted her sweater as she glanced again at the children. It looked like Cortney was trying to explain to Chenin just how to hold the Frisbee.

"Cold, Casey?"

She shook her head. "Not really." The air was cool, but not cold. She leaned back against the log behind them. Keir's arm came around her, drawing her closer to him. Contentment filled her with the gesture. Casey closed her eyes, listening to the pounding of the waves as they hit the shore. She heard the two children plop themselves in front of them and opened her eyes.

"Make a sand castle with me, Casey?" Chenin begged, touching her hand.

Casey groaned. "Chenin, I just finished eating."

"Old age setting in already?" Keir asked solemnly, as he, too, sat up. His eyes were twinkling.

Casey sent him an insulted look and stood, grabbing Chenin's hand. "Come on, Chenin. Old age indeed! At least I wasn't the one groaning for hours because I ate too much!"

"Hey, I only groaned once!" Keir called after her. "Okay, maybe it was twice!"

Casey laughed as she trudged away from him, looking for a place in the sand that wasn't overrun by other exuberant youths throwing beach balls, Frisbees, or whatnot.

Chenin pulled her to a stop. "Can we not build our sand castle here?"

Casey glanced around, checking for flying objects and then smiled at the girl. "Here is just fine."

Chenin beamed and immediately sat down and began leveling the sand. Casey sat down beside her, watching. The girl was definitely diligent in her work. She packed up the sides of her castle, checking and double checking each level before she added more sand on top to make the next.

"Can I help?"

Casey turned around to find the young girl who had pulled in with her family only an hour or so ago and were camping in the site next to theirs. The girl was about Chenin's age.

"Can she, Casey?" Chenin was eyeing the bucket the smaller girl held in her hand.

"Of course." Casey moved to make room for the girl. "Your name was..?"

"Sally," said the girl. "We're camping way over there." She pointed toward the campers.

"I am Chenin," Chenin said. "If you would want, you can begin placing buckets of sand on the corners of our sand castle?"

Sally nodded and began filling her bucket with sand. Casey sat and watched as the two girls worked together.

It wasn't long before they were both giggling and talking as if they had been old friends.

Casey's eyes roamed back to Keir. He was still sitting where she had left him, playing some sort of game with Cortney. He glanced up and their eyes met. Warmth spread through her as he smiled.

"Casey."

Casey brought her attention back to the girls. Chenin was looking over at her.

"Do you like our castle?"

Casey's eyes briefly ran over their large, solid sand castle. "I definitely do. Is it finished?"

"Yes," both girls said together, causing a fit of giggles.

"And just in time, too." An older girl had come up from behind Casey. She smiled briefly at Casey, but turned to the girls. "Come on, Sally. Mom says you have to come back. It's too dark to be out here now."

Sally stood with a shrug and a good-bye to Chenin and followed her sister back to her parents.

Chenin watched her go. "She was nice."

"Yes, she was," Casey said, glad to see Chenin had made a friend. She hoped that the family would be staying in the campground at least through tomorrow for Chenin's sake. Chenin needed to interact with children her own age.

Chenin gazed down at her sand castle. "Do you think the waves will come up and wash it away?"

"We'll have to wait and see," Casey stood and held her hand out. "Come on, Chenin. It is getting too dark to see much. We wouldn't want Keir to worry about us."

The girl slipped her hand into Casey's and began to walk by her side. "Casey?"

"What is it, Chenin?" Casey looked down. There was troubled sound to the girl's voice.

She stopped and swallowed. "Must I go to the talent corps here in America now?"

Casey stopped and squatted before the child, taking the girl's small hands in hers. She gave them a light squeeze. "I'm afraid we don't have a talent corps here in America."

"Then I will not have to go?" The girl sounded hopeful.

"No, you will not have to go."

The girl's hands squeezed into Casey's. "Then I could go to school like Cortney...and Sally?"

Casey grinned at her as she stood and again took her hand. "That you can."

"I have not been to school before," Chenin said with a skip as they continued back toward Keir and her brother.

Casey looked at her in surprise. "You haven't?"

"Only to the corps." She looked up at Casey. "We are taught many things in the corps, but it is not like Cortney's school."

Cortney's head rose as he caught his name as they approached, but he turned immediately back to the game he was playing with his cousin. Casey smiled at Keir and sat down in the sand near him pulling Chenin down beside her.

"What did you do in the talent corps, Chenin?"

Chenin ran her fingers through the sand in front of her. "We practiced very hard for the programs."

"What kind of programs?"

"It is like singing and dancing together, what we do in the corps."

Casey smiled at her. "Did you enjoy it?"

Chenin thought a minute. "Some of it I liked."

"They were not very nice if she did not do it correctly," Cortney said looking at his sister. "She would have to do it again and again."

"Well, she won't have to any longer," Keir said. He stood and pulled Chenin up into his arms. "Come on. Let's go sit by the fire. I can see plenty of marshmallows being eaten and we're missing out."

The large campfire was just that; large. Almost big enough to be called a bon-fire. The two children quickly grabbed the sticks offered them and a marshmallow each. Keir took the last stick offered and sat down beside Casey. He slipped a marshmallow on the end and placed it into the fire. It wasn't long before he was pulling it out again.

It was roasted to a perfect golden brown. Casey watched as he carefully removed it from the stick and held it up to her.

She reached out, but Keir moved it away. "No Casey," he whispered. "Let me."

Casey lowered her hand, and he moved the roasted marshmallow and held it against her lips. Casey opened her mouth, and he popped the warm morsel into it.

She closed her eyes, savoring the treat. "Just perfect," she said when she swallowed it.

Keir grinned and placed another onto his stick.

"I will do a marshmallow for you, Casey," Chenin said.

Cortney shoved the last of the marshmallow he had just roasted into his mouth. "So will I."

Keir shook his head. "That's not necessary. I will take care of Casey tonight." His eyes were sparkling as they flickered back to her. He grinned back at his cousins. "This way you can eat all the marshmallows you want," he whispered loudly.

Chenin laughed and kissed him on the cheek. "I will, Keir. I like marshmallows!"

For the next half hour the four of them sat and enjoyed the marshmallows as well as the singing that had started around the fire. Several guitars began playing along, and further down the sand, someone's tape deck wired into speakers could be heard blasting. Already couples were up dancing to the modern tunes of the sixties. Casey enjoyed every moment of it.

"Last one," Keir said bringing Casey's attention back around as he placed another marshmallow against her lips. He popped it into her mouth as her lips parted, then popped another into his own before gathering the sticks from Chenin and Cortney and handing them to the boy who was collecting them.

Chenin bent over and kissed him on the cheek. "Thank you, Keir."

"Hey, don't thank me. You and Cortney roasted your own marshmallows."

"Casey did not."

"No, she didn't, did she?" His sparkling eyes turned back to Casey. "Well, Casey, do I get a 'thank you' from you?"

"Well, if I have to." She leaned into him, intent on kissing his cheek, but Keir shifted and her lips landed on his. Warmth burst through her and she let her lips linger.

"Keir?"

He slowly withdrew from Casey. "Yes, Cortney?"

"What is it that they are doing?"

Keir pulled his eyes from Casey. "What?"

"Those people," the boy said, pointing to the couples dancing. "What is it they are doing?"

"Dancing."

"That is dancing?" There was disbelief in his young voice. The couples were not touching, just twisting and moving in all sorts of directions. None seemed to be doing the same thing. His eyes went to Casey for confirmation.

"They really are," she said. She climbed to her feet and took his hand. "Come on. It's fun. I'll teach you!"

Chapter SEVENTEEN

Chenin came to her feet as well. "You will teach me, too?"

Casey flickered a glance at Keir. "I'm sure your cousin would love to teach you."

"You bet." Keir grinned as he came surging to his feet. He picked up Chenin and followed Casey to the other dancers.

Casey took Cortney right into the midst of them. "Close your eyes, Cortney," she said. The boy obeyed her. "Now, feel the music. Not with your ears, but with your body."

She grinned at the look of concentration on the boy's face. "Relax, Cortney. Now let your knees move with the beat...that's the way!"

Cortney opened his eyes and grinned at her, his knees bouncing to the music. Casey laughed and began dancing to the fast beat. Cortney, with only a slight hesitation, began imitating her moves.

"I like your dancing!" he said as they finished their third song in a row.

Casey groaned and threw herself on the sand. "You're going to wear me out, Cortney."

"You are tired, Casey?"

"I'm just out of breath." She turned to find Keir coming up behind her. He, too, groaned as he plopped himself down. "Oh, my."

"Old age setting in already?" Casey asked solemnly.

He shook his head and laughed. "Not a chance, Casey."

"Of course not. Want to go back and dance?"

He groaned and sank back into the sand. "What I want is a long, cold drink."

Cortney was back up on his feet. "I will get it for you, Keir."

"And I will gladly let you. Thank you... And get a drink for Casey, too."

"I will. Come on, Chenin."

Casey watched as Cortney took off with Chenin at his heels.

Keir looked over at her. "Who taught you to dance?"

"Both Henry and Donald. They needed someone to practice with so they could impress the girls."

"You're good."

Her face flushed. "I enjoy it." She hadn't been aware that Keir had been watching her. "You're not too bad yourself."

"I'm out of practice." He sat up as Cortney returned with his soda. Casey watched as he popped the tab and took a long drink. Chenin crawled into her lap.

"Casey?"

"Yes?" she said bringing her eyes to the girl.

"I cannot get my drink open."

Casey reached down and took the can of soda from Chenin. Opening it, she returned it to the child.

She opened and took a long drink of her own soda. A contented breath came out of her.

"Keir?" Cortney's voice sounded troubled as he sat down beside his cousin.

"What is it, Cortney?"

"It is Casey," the boy said, surprising Casey. He was looking up at Keir. "Chenin says that she has no life-ring. It that true?" The boy's hand was fingering his own life-ring.

Keir nodded. "It is true."

"But how then, can she pledge her life in marriage?"

Keir flashed a glance in Casey's direction, but answered the boy seriously. "It is different here in America, Cortney. They do not exchange life-rings."

"How then, do they pledge themselves?"

"In America, when a man wants to marry a woman, he buys her what they call an engagement ring."

"It is not his?"

"Not as a life-ring is, no. But the ring he gives her is a symbol of his love. He chooses it for her alone. And if she accepts, she wears it on her hand."

Chenin stood up. "Keir, you will have to give an engage...an engage..." She stopped and attempted to start over. "You will have to give an engage ring?"

"No, Chenin," Keir said resolutely drawing the child to him. His glance flickered to Casey and back. "I will give my life-ring to the woman of my heart."

The child sighed in apparent relief. "I am glad, Keir."

A grin came out of him. "I am, too, *avi*." His glance flickered to the dancers, then to Casey. Moving Chenin, he stood and pulled Casey to her feet.

"Want to teach these two how to twist?"

A Chubby Checker song was blaring and Casey willingly complied. Within minutes the four of them were laughing and twisting in the sand with everyone else.

"This is fun!" Chenin was laughing as she tried to outdo her brother. Both were trying moves that Casey and Keir, as well as those dancing around them, were trying. Twice Cortney landed on his knees, and once flat on his bottom with Chenin on top of him. They both came up laughing as the song came to an end. It was replaced almost immediately by the slow, seductive voice of Elvis Presley. The two Thernian children sank back into the sand, groaning.

Grinning, Casey glanced up at Keir. He smiled and shrugged then held out his hands. "Dance with me, Casey?"

Casey's heart jumped as she willingly placed her hands into his and let him draw her to him. He slowly raised her hands to his shoulders then let his own slide down her back, drawing her close. His eyes met hers, suspending her in warm anticipation. He laced his fingers behind her, and pulled her closer still. Casey felt a feather light kiss on her forehead as they began swaying gently to the sensuous love song.

She laid her cheek against his chest, savoring the feel of being in his arms. Warmth was spreading through her; warmth, and a sweet, exquisite contentment. Her hands circled his neck, seemingly on their own accord, and she closed her eyes.

Enchantment. It was the only word she could think of to describe the sweet, wonderful awe she felt as Keir moved slowly to the music. She was being transported magically to the heavens and she wanted never to come down.

The song came to its heart-throbbing end, and she gave an inaudible sigh as she stilled, waiting for Keir to release her. Until he did, she was not about to move, for she was not ready to break the intimate bond that had sprung up between them.

But Keir merely tightened his hold around her and began to sway again to the faster beat of the next song, not letting her go. It was one of those songs that was neither fast nor slow, but somewhere in the middle. Casey didn't notice. Already she was floating back to the heavens…

"Casey?"

"Hmm?"

He stilled and wordlessly lifted her chin. His lips touched hers and spread into a warm kiss.

"Oh, my." She could feel its warmth down to her toes.

He gave a gentle laugh and wrapped an arm around her as he walked her back across the sand to his cousins. Already the song had changed to another. Picking Chenin up into his arms, he adjusted her to his hip and took Casey's hand in his. Casey found her other hand taken by Cortney as they walked slowly back to the van.

"Keir?"

"Yes, Cortney?"

"Thank you for taking us to the clambake, and for fixing the chain to my life-ring."

"My pleasure, Cortney. I'm glad you had fun." He unlocked the van and opened the door setting a very tired Chenin inside. "Would you see Chenin to bed for us, Cortney?" he asked the boy. "The beds are already set up."

Cortney nodded. "I will. Are you and Casey going to return to the clambake?"

Keir's head shook slightly. "No. Casey and I will be just outside here. You go to sleep. We'll be in soon."

The boy disappeared into the van with his sister, closing the door behind him and Keir turned to Casey. Wordlessly, he took her hand and drew her into the shadows of the lone tree before drawing her gently into his arms. Casey could feel her heart beating wildly.

"Keir?"

"Hush," he whispered as his lips descended to hers.

An incredible sweetness invaded Casey as Keir's lips leisurely explored hers. Her arms crept slowly up and around his neck and her eyes closed as she savored the warm feeling of completeness that stole over her. Her mouth opened to his. She felt their tongues intermingle as the kiss deepened; tasted the heady sweetness he gave as he took the sweetness she offered.

"Oh, Casey," he groaned against her lips, pulling her closer to him. Again his lips covered hers, now more insistent and hungry and full of wanting. His hands roamed. Shivers ran up and down her spine. She felt flushed, alive with emotion as he kissed her again, and then again and again.

At some point his hands slipped under her sweater, spreading against her bare skin as he let them explore. The intimate touch of them warmed her skin, melting her bones. She felt his fingers slide under her bra, touching the fullness of her breasts...and felt them suddenly still.

His head came to rest against her forehead and he let out a deep, tortured breath. "Casey," he managed huskily. "If I don't send you in right now, I'm likely to go further than either one of us should."

Casey wanted to protest. Her heart twisted with sweet torture as Keir slowly withdrew his hands from her and smoothed down her sweater. His eyes were still bright with passion as he gently cupped her face. "No arguments, Casey," he whispered shakily. "Please. Just go in, before I do what I desperately want to do...Please, Casey."

His mouth touched hers with a gentle breath of softness before he turned her toward the van and gave her a gentle shove.

Exquisite tears blurred Casey's eyes. She knew without a doubt she was in love with Keir Jairon.

Chapter EIGHTEEN

"Casey?"

Casey groaned but refused to pull herself from her dream. She was wrapped in Keir's warm embrace, his lips caressing her own…

"Casey!"

The insistence of Chenin's young voice slowly brought her awake. She sighed and opened her eyes. "Yes, Chenin?"

"Casey, can we go see if the waves washed away our sand castle?"

Casey rolled over and looked at the girl. She was sitting up, still in her sleeping bag, looking hopefully at her. She smiled at the girl. "You really want to?"

Chenin nodded and Casey sat up and grabbed the child from her sleeping bag, tickling her until she squirmed and giggled and threw her arms around Casey.

"You are such fun, Casey!"

Casey grinned. "So are you. What do you say we get dressed and go check out a sand castle?"

Chenin readily complied and they raced to get dressed. They were both laughing as they stepped out of the van. Keir and Cortney both looked up from the warm fire that Keir had started. Keir smiled and came to his feet.

"Good morning, *avi*." He offered Casey the cup of coffee he had just poured.

A warm flush spread across her cheeks. "Good morning…Have you heard anything from your parents yet?"

"Not as yet, but I expect a call soon, unless of course, they just show up."

"I hope they just show up," Casey said.

Keir nodded. "So do I."

Chenin shifted from one foot to another. Keir looked down at her. "What's up?"

"Casey and I are going to see if the waves have taken our sand castle."

"Oh, you are, are you?" His eyes flickered to Casey and he bent down to the child. "You just be sure that Casey doesn't get taken by the waves," he whispered loudly to the child. "Okay?"

Chenin giggled. "Okay."

Casey shook her head with a wry smile. "Thanks loads."

Chenin took her hand and began heading across the sand. Casey slowed her down immediately, sipping at the hot coffee that Keir had handed her. The girl let go of her hand and ran ahead, apparently eager to see if her sand castle was still standing.

It was, of sorts. Half of it had been eaten by the waves, and part of it had been stepped on. Only the eastern most wall of the sand castle still stood standing untouched by neither wave nor human foot. Chenin wanted to start repairs to it immediately but Casey forestalled her, reminding her that she and Cortney had not yet had their lessons with Keir, nor breakfast for that matter, and that their aunt and uncle would be arriving soon.

With a resigned sigh, Chenin followed Casey back to the van. Cortney was sitting by the fire but there was no sign of Keir.

"He went to the lodge to get something that he needed to fix us breakfast," Cortney informed them.

Casey snapped her fingers. "Did you remind him to get more butter?"

Cortney shook his head.

"I will go remind him," Chenin said immediately.

"No," Casey said, handing Chenin the empty coffee mug. "You stay here with Cortney. I'll go. I have to make a phone call to my cousin anyway."

Besides, a few minutes alone with Keir held promises.

But Keir wasn't in the lodge store when Casey made her way inside. "He's in the back on the phone," Andy told her when she asked if he had been by.

Casey thanked the lodge owner with a smile and made her way down the short hallway to the back where the phone was located. Keir was speaking into it, his back to her. She started to walk quietly toward him, but stopped as his conversation carried across the room to her.

"I know. She's been wonderful, Mom," he was saying into the phone. "She really has, and a great help…Yes…"

Casey stopped and flushed, then caught her breath at his next words.

"No, I don't believe there's any possibility of that," he said wrapping the cord around his finger. "She's known from the beginning that I'm getting married in the near future…"

She's known from the beginning…

Casey froze as pain shot through her; intense, overwhelming pain that expanded through her entire being. She backed out of the room, then turned and ran.

Keir was getting married…In the near future. How could she have forgotten? How could she have believed..?

His heart belonged to someone else. Casey sank down into the dry sand by the beach, too stunned to cry. She felt shattered and empty, and numb. How could she have forgotten she berated herself? How?

She took a deep, shuddering breath, and watched the never-ending waves as they hit the shore. It was awhile before she stirred. With a heavy sigh, she headed back to the lodge, checking for the nearest bus station. She couldn't stay. Not now. Not with Keir…

She pushed the unfinished thought away and concentrated on her phone call to the station. She wrote down the times offered, had a word with Andy, and slowly walked back to the van. Saying good-bye was going to be hard…very hard.

"Casey!"

She spied Chenin running toward her. Casey picked up the child and held her close. Chenin wiggled away. "Keir says breakfast is just about ready."

"Keir says breakfast *IS* ready," Keir said, sticking his head out the van door. He smiled at Casey then sent her a keener glance at her weak attempt to smile in return.

Casey immediately turned her attention back to the child. "Let's go wash up."

Breakfast was as noisy as ever, the children for once, not picking up on her misery. They were too excited hearing that their aunt and uncle were going to be arriving by late afternoon. Apparently they had flown into Eugene and were in the process of hiring a car to drive to the campground. Casey let the noise wash over and around her. Keir, she knew, had sent her several puzzled glances, but she avoided any contact with him. It hurt even to look at him and so she kept her head bent through most of the breakfast.

Cortney shoved away his plate. "Keir, can we go down to the beach before our lessons today?"

Casey stood and picked his plate up along with the other plates. It had fallen to her in the last few days to wash and clean up and at the moment, she was glad. It would give her an excuse to avoid Keir even longer.

"Not to swim," she heard Keir answer the boy. "It's still too cool outside." She turned toward the sink.

"Can we hunt for seashells?"

"I'll take you down shortly and then you can look for shells. Why don't you and Cortney go wait for me outside?"

With a quick kiss, the two children left happily enough and Keir turned to Casey. She started the water in the small sink and added the dishes. Keir came up quietly behind her.

"What is it, Casey? What's wrong? You hardly touched your breakfast, and you haven't said two words since you've come in."

Casey's heart stopped momentarily, turning painfully in her breast. She took a deep, silent breath. "I...I'm going home today, Keir; this afternoon. There's a bus that leaves for Salt Lake at one-thirty."

Stillness filled the van. "You're going home?" His voice held pained bewilderment.

"Yes." It was barely a whisper.

Again there was a long moment of silence. "What about the kids?"

"They've got you," she said staring at a fly buzzing noisily around the sink. "Besides, your parents will be here for them this afternoon."

She heard Keir take in a deep, pain-filled breath. "I thought you wanted to meet them?"

"I know, I did, but…" Even another day would be too much. "I've got to go, Keir! I've stayed too long already."

"Casey…"

"Don't!" she cried painfully. "Don't ask me to stay because I can't. I've got to go. Now!"

Stillness again filled the van. She heard him shift his feet and prayed that he wouldn't touch her, wouldn't try and turn her around. He didn't.

"Do you have enough money?" he asked at last.

"I'll get by."

"You don't want to fly home?"

Casey shook her head. She wished she could, it would take less time to get home, but the thought of being in a plane still shattered her nerves.

"Casey…"

"Keir, don't. Please."

"All right." She could feel his bewilderment. A moment went by. A breath escaped him. "I'll see to your bus ticket."

"It's not necessary."

"I know," he said quietly, "but I'll see to it just the same."

Casey swallowed. "All right…Thank you."

Again silence. She wanted him to go, to leave her alone. She needed to be alone…

She heard him walk toward the door. The catch clicked. He was going. She spun around. "Keir."

"We'll tell them later. You finish up in here and then come join us. Spend the next few hours with us."

Casey nodded, and he, with a slight, off-balance smile, left her alone. She finished the dishes and put them away, brushing diligently at the tears that were falling.

She didn't want to go. But she couldn't stay. She had stayed too long already. Chenin and Cortney were already too attached to her. And she was too attached to Keir. She couldn't bear to have him find out how she felt, not after hearing what she had heard.

With a heart-rending breath, she attempted to pull herself together. They were waiting for her. If she didn't join them soon they would come looking for her. She wiped her eyes on one of the towels.

It's for the best, she told herself fiercely, for everyone.

Chenin and Cortney were in the process of building another sand castle with the added help of Sally and her bucket. Keir sat nearby watching, not the children, but the waves that were crashing on the shore. He sent her a wan smile as she sat down near him. His voice was soft.

"Are you all right?"

She stared out at the vast ocean. She wasn't all right. He was in love with someone else. He was going to marry someone else. How could she be all right? "I'm all right."

"Casey…"

"Don't Keir."

"Is it because of last night?"

She shook her head. It was, and it wasn't, but the line between the two was too fine to distinguish. "I have to be at work on Monday, and the bus won't get me there until Sunday," she said instead.

Keir reached over and took her hand before she could stop him. A shudder ran through her. Not wanting to fight him, not wanting him to let go, she let her hand remain in his. Besides, it would be for the last time.

The sand castle was eventually finished, the weather warmed, and the two children, tired of playing in the sand, begged to go swimming. Casey again agreed, though she spent more of her time watching the two children and Keir splashing in the surf than swimming herself. She would have to leave soon, she knew, but she found it impossible to make her excuses and go pack. It was Keir who finally called a halt.

Cortney protested. "Just a little longer, Keir?"

"Maybe later," Keir said, throwing him a towel.

"I am hungry," Chenin said as she wrapped herself in a towel of her own.

"Then let's go eat."

They ate a light meal of sandwiches and chips outside on the picnic table, though once more, Casey found that she could eat little. The two children again seemed not to notice, and Keir, though she knew he did notice, said nothing.

"Keir, cannot we go buy an ice cream?" Chenin asked when she was done eating, "For…dessert?"

He nodded. "I'm sure we can." He looked to Casey.

"You go ahead," she said a touch too brightly. "I'll just clean up and go…change."

"But I will help you clean up." Chenin was already on her feet.

"That's all right, Chenin. You go have ice cream with Keir and Cortney. I'll clean up today."

"But I do not mind!"

"Chenin." It was Keir who stopped her. His voice was quiet as he held his hand out to her. "Let's go get that ice cream."

"Okay," the girl said, looking puzzled. She looked back at Casey. "But I will come right back to help you."

Casey managed to smile as they skipped off with Keir. With a heavy heart, she gathered up the dirty dishes, and headed back into the van. Chenin did not come back to help.

So Keir must have told them. Casey wiped away the tears gathering in her eyes. It wouldn't do any good to cry. She had to go. Had to.

But it hurt, and the tears came anyway, and this time Casey let them fall. She washed and dried the dishes, then picked up the van before turning at last to her packing. She was sitting on the picnic table waiting with her suitcase beside her when Keir finally returned with his cousins.

No one wanted to say good-bye. They took a last walk along the beach, but no one played with the waves or looked for shells.

"I'd better go," she said at last. "Andy said he'd get someone to drive me in."

"We're driving you in," Keir said. "Andy offered us the use of his car." Casey didn't argue.

It was a silent ride to the bus station located in the nearby town. Keir settled her and the children on one of the benches while he purchased her ticket and bought her several magazines and a sack lunch. "Your bus leaves in fifteen minutes," he told her.

It was the shortest fifteen minutes Casey had ever not wanted to wait for. All too soon she was standing at the door with Chenin's arms wrapped around her waist. "I want to come with you," the child cried.

Casey bent down and hugged her close, feeling her heart breaking all over again. Her own voice cracked. "I know, love," she whispered unsteadily, "but Cortney needs you and you must take care of Keir."

Chenin's arms only tightened as she began to sob.

Casey wanted to cry herself. "Oh, Chenin. It won't be forever. I promise. I'll see you and Cortney again. I will." She hugged the girl tighter. "Please, Chenin," she whispered, "Take care of Keir and Cortney for me until I can come back. All right?"

The child's arms held her tightly a moment longer, then slowly withdrew. "All right," she gulped wiping at her tears. "But you come back soon."

Next it was Cortney; small, brave, dependable Cortney. He took both her hands and squeezed them tightly. "I have something for you," he told her. He slowly removed his medallion from around his neck. "I think Father would want you to have it after all you have done." The boy solemnly placed it over her head and then unable to control himself any longer, he too, flung his arms around her, hugging her tightly. "I love you, Casey."

"I love you, too, Cortney, both you and Chenin. She hugged them again then stood and turned to Keir. A single tear had begun to slide down her cheek and he reached up and gently wiped it away.

"You take care."

Casey managed a nod. "Will you write?" she asked with tremendous effort, "Let me know when they're safe and settled?"

"Yes, Casey, I promise you. I'll write." He took her hands and kissed them one at a time, then bent and kissed her gently, tenderly on the lips.

"K'avii-tae, sher'avi," he whispered. He pressed something into the palm of her hand, closing her hand around it, but gave Casey no time to wonder about it as his lips once more took hers, deeply this time; longingly.

Casey managed to pull herself from him. "Take care," she whispered as she turned and ran blindly for the bus.

She watched them – Cortney, Keir, and Chenin – standing hand in hand, as the bus pulled out into the road…Watched them until the bus turned, and she could see them no more.

Only then did she open her hand and find the small, white-gold ring attached to its silver chain.

Keir's life-ring.

Chapter NINETEEN

Casey's heart turned over as she stared at the ring in disbelief.

His life-ring; the ring promised to the woman of his heart…And he had placed it in her hand; given it to her.

"Oh, Keir," she cried softly. "You shouldn't have." For it could not possibly mean what it implied. It was his way of showing his heartfelt gratitude as was the medallion Cortney had given her. It had to be! Yet…

No, Chenin. I will give my life-ring to the woman of my heart.

Her heart thudded as she again heard the solemn resoluteness of Keir's voice. It had been a vow; a promise to the woman he loved.

And he had given it to her.

But how could it possibly mean what it implied? He had told them in the beginning that his heart was already taken; had even described his future wife to her with loving conviction!

And he had told his mother, *just this morning,* that he was marrying soon.

Yet he had given his life-ring to her and had kissed her like he never wanted to let her go.

Casey swallowed, her heart thudding painfully inside her chest with both awe and despairing doubt. She closed her hand around the ring and held it where Keir had placed it; held it in the palm of her hand for the entire length of her journey.

It was a journey she had no desire to be traveling and wanted desperately to halt; a journey she was afraid to call a halt to. For despite what her heart was telling her, her mind filled her with insecure doubts.

If he had really meant it for what it implied, why hadn't he said something? Because it didn't mean what she wanted it to mean? Because he really was in love with someone else? Then why had he kissed her like he did, and why so often?

Why had he told his mother that she had known from the beginning he was getting married soon?

Casey determinedly pushed such conflicting fears and doubts and questions aside. She didn't want to think about them. Instead she brushed the tears that stung her eyes away and simply concentrated on the ring in her hand; on Keir. He said he would write. He promised he would. She would wait for his letter…and then all her doubts and fears and questions would be put to rest.

Because then she would know.

The bus didn't pull into Saltine until early Sunday morning. Casey tiredly found a taxi and went on home.

The phone in her apartment was ringing when she finally arrived. Her heart jumped as she immediately thought of Keir. But it wasn't Keir. Her cousin's voice was on the line, as well as a good amount of static. The phone line appeared even worse than before she had left.

"Criminy, Casey! When are they going to get those phone lines fixed over there? This is the first time I've been able to get through to you and I can barely hear you!"

Casey shook her head. "I'm sorry. Apparently the phone lines are even…" She stopped as the static suddenly cleared. "Donald?"

"I'm here. At least the static has stopped. Where have you been, anyway? I've been over there trying to get hold of you for the last two days. I thought you had to be back to work Thursday?"

"I got it extended," she said ignoring his question. "I'll be back at work tomorrow."

"I should hope so. Rent doesn't grow on trees. At least you're back. I was hoping and praying you would be."

Casey was wishing she wasn't. She was wishing she was still in Turtle Sands, in Keir's arms…

"Casey!"

"I'm sorry, Don. I take it you called for your car."

"Not actually. Have you gotten your own back yet?"

"Not yet. I planned to check on it during my lunch break tomorrow."

"Then keep my car for a while. I don't need it anyway. Not right away."

"Why's that?"

"Because I just bought myself a new one."

"You bought a new car?"

"I bought a new car. I thought I'd celebrate the fact that I just got a promotion."

"A promotion? You got a promotion?"

"A good one." She could hear the grin in his voice.

"That's wonderful, Don."

"I'll agree with that! But it's going to mean a lot of traveling for the first month or so, which brings me to why I called. Could you do me a favor?"

The phone suddenly spit out a bout of static, then receded.

"Donald? What were you saying?"

"Could you take care of Swashbuckler for me for the next day or two?"

"Swashbuckler? Donald, you know I can't have him here." They didn't allow pets in her building whatsoever, especially dogs and cats, and Swashbuckler was her cousin's treasured tabby cat. "Why isn't Amanda watching him for you?" Amanda was Donald's neighbor who often watched Swashbuckler for him when he went out of town.

"Amanda and her family have left for the week so I've got no one else to watch him. Could you come over here every day and see that he's fed, maybe visit with him awhile? I can't find anyone else I trust to take him."

Casey bit back her sigh. "I'll be glad to, Donald."

Relief filled his voice. "You're one in a million, Casey. I'll leave his food out on the table."

"Donald!" she cried, realizing he was ready to hang up. "When are you leaving?"

"In about fifteen minutes," he said with a laugh. "I'm not sure when I'll be back, hopefully by Wednesday. Thank you, Coz, and I'll see you soon."

"Drive safe," Casey told him and rang off. She had just turned away when the phone rang again. She stared at it in surprise wondering if Donald had forgotten something. She again picked up the receiver.

"Miss Hammond? Casey Hammond?" Static intermixed with her name.

"Yes?" she said hesitantly, unable to recognize the voice through the static.

There was a slight hesitation from the other end, then, "This is Karl – Karl Banning. I don't know if you remember me, but…"

"Of course I remember you," Casey said. "What can I do for you, Karl?"

Again there was a slight hesitation. Or was it just that the static was getting worse this time?

"Would you repeat that, Mr. Banning?" She was unsure if he had spoken at all. "I've got problems with my phone."

"Did Keir happen to give you his or his parent's address?"

"I'm afraid he didn't." The ache in her heart immediately swelled. "You don't have it?"

"No," she heard the older man answer, "You see, I've just received, rather Dajon has just received, an important looking letter from Thern. I'd like to get it to him as soon as possible."

A letter from the children's father?

"Oh, Karl. Keir promised to write to me. Sometime within the next couple of days," she said. "If you give me your phone number, I'll call you as soon as I've heard from him."

Again a hesitation. "You don't know where he is now?"

Casey shook her head. "I'm afraid I don't. The kids met their uncle at a campground in Oregon. They should be on their way home. I'll make sure I call you as soon as I hear anything."

"You do that," Karl said, giving her his unlisted phone number. "You'll call right away?"

"As soon as I hear from him," Casey said. Then, "Karl, did the nadarb ever come back?"

There was hesitation again, slightly longer this time, and Casey wondered if he had heard her. But then came, "No Casey. They haven't come back. You said a letter should arrive any day?"

"Any day."

But two long weeks went by with no letter. No phone call. Nothing. It was as if the children and Keir had never existed. Only the medallion and the small, white-gold ring told her otherwise.

There was little incident during the two weeks. No nadarb came as Casey had half-feared. Although there was the day she had been sure her apartment had been searched. Nothing was missing, and everything had remained as she had left it, but she still sensed invasion. Nerves, she had told herself.

She occupied her time with Swashbuckler whenever Amanda couldn't watch him, with Donald when he was in town, as well as with work. She hadn't been reprimanded for the two days she had missed, most likely due to the fact that she had made it back by the stipulated Monday. Her job was still hers.

Casey also spent her time fighting the landlord and the telephone company for a new phone line. Her phone had begun working only intermittently and the static was bad when it did.

Still, despite how busy she kept herself, she missed Keir and Chenin and Cortney dreadfully though she tried not to dwell on Keir. He would write. He had promised, just as soon as the children were secure and settled. But the fact he hadn't worried her. Had something happened? Had Bruen and his foreign thugs found them before they could legalize everything? Were they on the run again? Was it simply that things were taking time?

Or was it the fact that Keir had simply decided not to.

Casey shook her head as she reached up and touched the life-ring she now wore constantly around her neck. Her own small baby ring lay on the silver chain beside it. She had placed it there that first day she had arrived home. It was an admission, she acknowledged, of her love…and of her hope and belief that he would write, or call. Just as soon as the children were settled.

But what was taking so long? It had already been two weeks without a letter or a word from him. Two long weeks!

"Oh, stop it!" she vocally admonished herself climbing out of bed.

She should be glad, she told herself forcefully. Keir Jairon was a chauvinist! He believed woman was made for man; believed in a woman's 'rightful place' and would expect her to want to stay in it! Fat chance! She didn't need or want that.

Or so she told herself.

Not that it helped. She couldn't quite rid herself of his warm, smiling eyes, or his gentle touch…or the feel of his arms secure around her and of the warm kisses he so freely gave. She couldn't forget his humor or his caring concern or his solid strength.

Nor could she forget the significance of the life-ring he had placed in her hand...

A heartfelt groan escaped her. "Oh, Keir," she called out to him. "Don't do this to me!"

She showered and dressed then reached for the medallion. Her heart caught and thudded painfully. Cortney's medallion was no longer where she had remembered placing it. All thoughts fled from Casey except one. Where was the medallion?

It wasn't on her dresser. Hadn't she always placed it on the dresser? Her hand went unconsciously to Keir's life-ring and the even smaller ring beside it. Both rested safely on the silver chain around her neck. But Cortney's medallion was nowhere to be seen.

Casey tore her apartment apart and put it back together again but the medallion did not surface. Had it broken loose, then? She began to retrace her steps of the day before; the library, the grocery store, the offices at work. No one had seen the silver medallion.

She cleaned out the cars, her own and Donald's, for she had been using them both. Yet, though she combed the front and back seats of each, she found no medallion.

It was gone and Casey's depression doubled. With a heavy sigh, she retrieved the mail from her box and sank down on her sofa. No letter. Only a short note from Henry:

Casey

What are you and Donald up to? I've called you both but get no answer. Wanted to let you know we found a home right outside of Fairbanks. It's a beautiful four bedroom home so there's plenty of room for you to come visit. You can come enjoy the Northern Lights with us. In the meantime here's our phone number. Please give it to Don and have him call me as soon as possible. I need to talk to him before Friday. Thanks, Henry

Friday. And it was already late Wednesday afternoon. She sighed heavily and trudged downstairs to the pay phone across the street knowing her own phone was totally out of service; had been for two days now. The phone lines in the entire apartment complex were finally being replaced by the phone company. At least something positive was happening, she mumbled, dialing Donald's number.

Donald gave a laugh when he got the message. "I just got the same letter. Sounds ominous. I wonder what he wants."

"Call him and see."

"I was just about to." He shifted subjects. "But before I forget, would you be willing to bring my car on over?"

"What happened to your new car?"

"My new car's fine. I just thought it was time to clean up the old one. I might have a buyer for it. So will you? I'll fix us dinner."

Casey shrugged unconsciously. "Dinner sounds fine."

"Good. I'll see you later."

asey rang off, and made her way back up to her apartment. She found her wallet then picked up her keys, as well as the keys to Donald's car. With a backward glance to her apartment, she locked her door and left. Ten minutes later she was standing on the front steps of the small house that once belonged to her brother as well as her cousin. Now it belonged to just Donald.

"Hey, I didn't mean drop everything and run," Donald said greeting her.

"I was hungry," she said with a shrug. She shoved the keys into the pocket of her jeans then bent and scratched Swashbuckler who had come up to her. The cat meowed and sauntered off and Casey walked into the kitchen where Donald had returned to his dinner preparations. "Did you talk to Henry?"

"I did."

"So what did he want?"

He glanced at her. "He needed a file sent up to him that he left behind. I've already got it in an envelope and ready to be dropped in the mail...How about a glass of wine?" he offered, glancing at her again.

"I think I'd like that," she said sitting down on a nearby stool.

Donald poured them both a glass of wine, handed hers to her, and then went on with his preparations. Casey watched him in silence. Donald, unlike most men she knew, loved to cook and was superb at it. It was he, rather than her mother, who had taught her most of what she knew about cooking. Tonight's meal, she noted, was a simple one; minute steaks, steamed vegetables, and broiled potatoes.

"It's a good thing Henry doesn't get married and leave for Alaska every week," he said, interrupting her thoughts.

She managed a brief smile. "It's not Henry, Don. The North Pole and Janet are welcome to him."

"Then what is it?"

Casey fingered her wine glass. "It's just that I lost something that, well…that was rather special to me."

"A man?" It came ever-so-lightly.

Casey felt her face flush. "No. A necklace or rather a silver medallion." She let out a heavy sigh. "I've looked everywhere."

Donald glanced up. "The one you were wearing last week?"

"Yes."

Her cousin leaned across the counter and added more wine to her glass. "You'll find it, Casey. I know you will. Just drop it from your mind for now, and smile…and tell me you brought my car."

"I brought your car," she said.

A grin came out of him. "Good. Want to help me clean it out and wash it later? I need it ready to go."

"Who's buying it?"

"Emily's brother." Emily was his current girlfriend. "He'd like to get his hands on it sooner than later."

"I suppose I can help you then." It at least would give her something to do; something to concentrate on.

He turned back to his dinner. "How's work going?"

Casey shrugged. "Work is work."

"Bored with it?"

Casey shrugged again.

"Hey, you can always start looking for something else. Knowing you, you'll find something you want sooner or later."

Casey had found what she wanted, and she wanted it sooner, not later!

Donald handed her the silverware. "Set the table for us, will you? You know where everything else is."

Casey took the silverware from him and set it on the small dining table. She found glasses and napkins then sat down. Donald dished up two plates and set one down in front of her.

"It looks wonderful, Donald."

"It should. I always give it my best." He saluted her with his wine glass and began to eat. "Tell me about your medallion, Casey."

Casey shrugged. "There's not much to tell. It's silver, about the size of a silver dollar, with beautiful scrolled etchings on it."

He stopped eating and studied her a moment. "How did it come to mean so much to you?"

"Because Cortney gave it to me."

"Cortney?" Her cousin's eyes flashed.

"A ten year old boy," she retorted. She sighed and looked down at her plate. "I met him at the airport, right after you had taken off; him and his sister. They were looking for their uncle."

"Did you find the uncle for them?"

Casey shook her head. "Not exactly. Cortney had his address in Brickett, but when we got there we found that he had moved. Then, well, in a round-about way I helped them find their cousin. He's seeing to it that they get to his father."

"And Cortney gave you the medallion in gratitude. Why is it, Casey, that I have this odd feeling that there's a lot you aren't telling?"

Casey flushed. "I'm sorry, Donald. It's just…"

"Hey," he stopped her reaching across the table. "It's all right. I don't have to know."

Casey remained silent a moment. "Have you ever heard of a country called Thern?"

"It's a small soviet country near Sweden, isn't it?"

"Actually it was overtaken by the soviets twenty-eight years ago. Chenin and Cortney were just smuggled out of there."

Donald's eyes came up in evident interest.

A deep breath escaped her. "In actual fact, they ran away while they were in California, on some sort of talent tour. Their father had arranged it. He gave Cortney his uncle's address and told him what to do. And it worked, or would have worked, except Dajon, Cortney's uncle, no longer lived at that address."

"And that's where you came in."

She sent her cousin a brief smile. "I actually came in before that." Casey with another deep breath sat back and began describing how Cortney and Chenin had approached her, and the events that had since followed, omitting only the details of her abduction by Bruen and the relationship that had sprung up between her and Keir.

"Oh, Donald!" she cried in the end, "I'm worried about them. Keir promised to write as soon as they were safe with his father. That was over two weeks ago!"

"Give him time, Casey," her cousin said. "Maybe he's waiting until the legalities of it are straightened out."

"Or maybe he decided it wasn't worth his while," she muttered.

Donald eyed her a moment then grinned. "Come on. How about taking your frustrations out on cleaning and washing a car?"

Casey grudgingly joined him and together they began to go through the car. Donald took the front seat and Casey began cleaning and washing down the back. Again she kept her eyes out for the silver medallion.

Donald stopped her a short while later. "Want anything to drink?"

Casey shook her head.

"Hey, cheer up!"

"Oh, Donald! I just have to find that medallion!"

"You will. You just wait and see." Donald pulled her from the car and set her down on the front steps. He disappeared into the house then came back out a moment later and handed her a can of cold soda. "You've become rather attached to those two kids," he said off-handedly.

"I know." She unconsciously reached up and touched the life-ring.

"And the cousin?" His voice was light.

Casey flushed and brought her hand down. "Keir's already got a girl." At least it was beginning to look that way, she thought in unhappy frustration.

"I'm sorry."

Casey set down the soda and turned to her cousin fighting again all her misery and frustration and worry. "There's nothing to be sorry about! That man is impossible; a true chauvinist! Do you know, he actually believes a woman has her *place*! Of all the insufferable, outrageous, chauvinistic--"

"Wonderful, brilliant ideas," Donald finished. He grinned at her.

Her misery and frustration grew. "You men are all alike!" She came to her feet. "I'm going to go clean out your trunk!"

With that, she stomped off from the front steps and out to the driveway, pulling Donald's car keys from her pocket. Her own keys came out with them and landed on the cement pavement. "Great!"

Donald, who had followed, shook his head. "Temper, temper." He set down the box he had picked up and brought over. "I want to take everything out of it and then you can give it a good vacuuming before I put anything back in."

Casey said nothing as she retrieved her keys from the pavement, shoving them back into her pocket before she opened the trunk of her cousin's car.

"How is it?" Donald asked.

"Not bad." The trunk was basically empty outside of a paper bag and the four books she had purchased at the used book store next to the library. She had forgotten she had bought them; forgotten she had even put them into the trunk. She started gathering them up. "I've only got to…"

She stopped and gave a small cry as her eyes caught sight of a familiar chain. Still attached to it was the silver medallion. "Donald! It's here!" she cried out.

"What?"

"The medallion!" Elation filled her as she dropped the books and picked it up. "The chain must have snapped when I put in the books." She held it out for Donald to see and it slipped from the chain. Her elation died as the medallion cracked on the pavement and came apart.

"Oh, no!" She bent and immediately picked up the two halves.

But Donald was studying a small, shiny chip that had slipped from the medallion's insides.

"Casey." He stood up slowly, the chip in his hand. "Unless I miss my guess, this is some sort of computer chip."

"Computer chip?"

"Computer chip," Donald repeated. He looked up and met her startled eyes. "You said their father was a scientist?"

"Working on some kind of new fuel." She stared up at her cousin. "Donald, do you think this could be the finished formula?"

"It just could be." He took the medallion from her hand and studied it a moment. "It didn't break, Casey. It fits together like…this!" He snapped the two pieces back together, hiding the computer chip inside it once again.

Casey took it from him. "And I bet Cortney didn't even know the chip was there." She looked up at her cousin. "Don! We've got to get this to his uncle. What if Keir doesn't write?"

"Don't you have *any* idea how to reach him?"

"None!" Casey almost cried. "Not even Karl Banning knows how to get in touch with him. Nor would the campground where we had been. All I know is that he lives somewhere in…" She stopped suddenly and looked at her cousin. "Raccoon Creek. It's in Idaho. Keir says his father camps there consistently; his dad's home away from home. Maybe someone up there would know how to get in touch with him."

"It's a starting point," Donald said. "Come on." He pulled her back inside the house and she watched in puzzlement as he went through the box of books he pulled from his closet. "Here they are," he said, pulling out two.

They were campground books of the entire Western states. "You take that one, I'll take this one," he told her. For the next twenty minutes the only sound was that of turning pages. It was Donald who found it.

"You're right. It is in Idaho, Casey, in the Smoke River Mountains. Not too far from Yellow Pine." He studied the map on the previous page. "It doesn't look too hard to get to. All we have to do is take Highway 93 up to Stanley, then this small highway the rest of the way."

He sent her a smile. "I'll tell you what. We'll give your Keir until Saturday, to write. If he hasn't written by then, we'll go up to this Raccoon Creek and trace him and his father from there. Okay?"

Casey gave her cousin an impulsive hug. "Thank you, Donald. Thank you, thank you!" She pulled herself away and shoved Cortney's medallion into the pocket of her jeans. "I suppose that means we had better get that car of yours finished so you can get it sold before we have to leave."

They worked until the car was cleaned, washed, and polished. Donald grinned at his cousin. "At least that's done. Want to stay around for a while? I've got popcorn and ice cream...or would you rather I take you home?"

"Could you take me home?" she said. It was nearly nine and there was a program on television she wanted to watch, one she knew her cousin definitely wouldn't be interested in. Besides, she was tired. "I'll go get my wallet and the envelope for Henry," she told him, dashing back inside the house.

Donald was already backing out his car when she returned. It was a new sports Jaguar, a candy apple red in color. Casey again marveled over it. Donald opened the passenger door for her.

"You mean you're not going to let me drive?"

"Get in."

"Seriously," she said climbing in beside him. "Aren't you ever going to let me drive it?"

"Casey, I haven't even had it a month yet and already you want to take it off my hands!"

"Well, you have to admit, it's the right car to take off your hands."

"Not from my point of view."

Casey sniffed. "Some cousin you are."

"The best you've got." He drove quietly for several blocks, dropped the envelope off in the mailbox in front of the post office then drove on. He eventually turned the corner and pulled up behind her car that was parked on the street. "How's the old pony getting along?" he said indicating her mustang.

"Wonderful now," she replied climbing out of the Jaguar. "Vince finally solved its problems, replaced some parts, and gave it a good tune-up...Thanks for the lift, Donny."

"All right, you!" He stopped suddenly, all teasing gone. "Casey, did you leave your apartment open?"

Casey's stomach lurched as her eyes flew to her upstairs apartment. Her lights were on and her door was swung open. "No...Donald?"

"Come on." He was out of the car leading her cautiously toward the staircase. "You stay here," he ordered.

Casey was about to disobey and follow him up the stairs when she heard movement on the landing above them, then voices; Bruen's voice.

She didn't wait. "Donald, run!" she cried out.

Donald turned, but already Casey was racing toward her car.

"*CASEY!*"

Chapter TWENTY-ONE

Casey glanced up fleetingly as she hurriedly unlocked her car door. Bruen was standing on the landing, the man beside him pointing her out. Then he was moving, charging down the stairs, pushing Donald out of the way…

Casey slid into her car and locked her door, throwing her wallet on the passenger's seat. There was the sound of a gun, and a dull thud as something hit her trunk but she paid no attention. Her engine roared to life, and with her foot on the floor, the little mustang shot out into the street and around the corner.

She had no conscious thought of where she was going. Only that she had to go, and keep going. She kept her eyes glued to the streets and pushed her car over the speed limit. She thought fleetingly of Donald, wondering if he had been hurt or if Bruen would go after him, but dismissed the worry. Bruen had no reason to want Donald. Just her.

She found herself on the freeway when the initial fear faded, in the heart of Salt Lake City. It was dark and the traffic was almost light. She dared a glance in her rear view mirror but it was impossible to tell.

Had she lost them? Or did one of those headlights belong to Bruen's car? She changed lanes and sped up but no car seemed to follow. She kept going…tried it again. Still no change in the traffic behind her.

She didn't relax. She edged her car into the right lane, then off the freeway and stopped at the end of the off ramp. She waited but no car followed. Another minute ticked by. The light changed from green, to red, and to green again.

Feeling steadier, she edged her mustang back on the freeway. She had only a half a tank of gas, but she dared not stop. Not yet. She could stop for gas in one of the smaller towns further north.

North.

She was heading for Raccoon Creek. She had done it unconsciously. She only hoped she would remember the right highway when she came to it. Maybe the service station attendant would have a map where she stopped.

She put her hand over her pocket, making sure the medallion was still safe inside. It's what Bruen was now after. She didn't know how she knew, she just knew that somehow, some way, he had discovered the existence of the computer chip.

She didn't think for a minute that he knew she had the medallion. It was the boy's and she was his link to the boy. But Bruen being Bruen, left no stone unturned. He had searched her apartment for it. Thoroughly. Just to be certain. Now he was after her.

Casey looked again in her rear-view mirror. They were out of the city now and there were fewer cars. It looked safe enough, but it was impossible to tell. The cars behind her were only dark shapes with glowing eyes… Blinding eyes.

She didn't take any chances. She kept her foot on the accelerator, still going as fast as she dared.

The freeway climbed in elevation and she shifted gears. She passed one town, then another. She would have to get gas soon. It would do no good to run out with Bruen somewhere behind her.

The town of Portage came and Casey, with trepidation, pulled off the freeway. Almost immediately, a car sped up and exited behind her. Casey's stomach lurched. She stepped down on the accelerator and shot through the red light and back on the freeway. The car didn't follow. Out of the corner of her mirror, she saw it turn and make its way down a side street.

She drove past several more exits then tried again. No car followed her this time. She found a service station and had the water and oil checked, as well as the tank filled, while she forced herself to go into the small store inside the station. She wasn't hungry, but she was tired. Having something to eat or drink in the car would help her to stay awake. She purchased several varieties of chips, a few candy bars, and soda. Soda had caffeine in it, and she needed the caffeine in order to stay awake.

At the last minute, Casey bought a pound bag of ice. There was an old half broken Styrofoam ice chest outside the door. Casey picked it up and put it in the front seat of her mustang, buckling it down so it wouldn't tip. She added the bag of ice and the sodas, and after a trip to the ladies room and a glance at the map, she was off again.

She had only to stay on the freeway to the state highway and then stay on that until Stanley. Then she would be on the smaller mountain highway leading to Raccoon Creek…and Keir.

Her hand went unconsciously to his life-ring. She didn't wonder anymore if he would be happy to see her. It was enough that she would find him.

Her mustang climbed through one summit, then another, and then there was a long downhill stretch before they began climbing again. Casey glanced at her watch. It was past 12:30 and she was finding it difficult to stay awake. She felt cramped and stiff and knew she had to get out of the car, even if it was only for a few minutes. She would take the next rest stop.

The rest stop was surprisingly empty. She climbed out of her car, stretched, then walked around the small building several times before she used the restroom facilities. Coming out, she stopped and studied the map attached to the wall.

Twin Falls was only an hour further up the road. If she hadn't spotted Bruen by then, she would stop there for the night. She dug out a can of soda from the battered ice chest and opened it, then walked around to check out the damage to her mustang. She had heard the bullet hit, but where?

The bullet hole was on the side of her trunk, much larger than she would have expected. Thank God it hadn't hit elsewhere! She stared at it a moment, then turned away, and with a heavy breath, leaned against the back of her car.

She felt the crisp coolness of the air, could smell the fresh pine as she forced herself to finish her soda. She glanced up. The stars were so close she felt she could reach out and touch them. A beautiful night, she sighed, but quiet...eerily quiet. She shivered.

Her eyes wandered back toward the direction she had come and her heart jolted. Coming down the mountain she could see a car moving fast. There was no shape to it; no color. Just its two headlights and a single golden parking light.

She thought fleetingly of Donald, but knew it wasn't him racing down on her. The car was too wide to be Donald's; its headlights too dim. Her heart began to pound. There was no reason to believe it was Bruen or his men. Quite possibly it was just someone in a hurry.

But she knew.

The can of soda dropped from her hand as she ran back to her car. The way they were moving they would be upon her in minutes. She started her car and raced back onto the freeway, wishing desperately she hadn't stopped. She wasn't tired anymore, fear had taken care of that, but she still shouldn't have stopped. She should have known. *She should have known!*

She glanced out her rear view mirror and her foot pushed harder on the accelerator. The car, still impossible to tell its color, size, or make, was still coming, but slower now. They were climbing again. Casey gave her mustang a fond pat.

"Come on, pony." It was a good car, already five years old, but still in top condition and full of power. It flew over the mountain freeway just as fast as Casey allowed. The car behind her was no longer gaining, but then neither was it falling behind.

Their speeds had evened out with only a short half-mile between them. At least Casey judged it to be a half-mile. She raced on, keeping her eyes on the road and on the rear view mirror. She would have to lose them somehow, before she turned onto the smaller highway. It was not freeway, and it would slow her considerably, giving them the chance they needed to catch her.

But the turn-off came and still they were behind her. All hope that she had been wrong about it being Bruen vanished as he shot after her onto the highway. At least he hadn't gained...or had he? It was hard to tell. The highway, unlike the freeway, twisted with more regularity. It was darker too, making it impossible to judge the turns with top speed. At least the turns were banked; the highway in excellent condition.

Casey continued to push on. She passed one town then another, her speed increasing whenever it was possible. It was almost two in the morning but Casey was hardly aware of the time. All thought was on her driving, of making Stanley far enough ahead of them to lose them before she made her final turn.

But it was impossible. Bruen's car stuck behind her as if an invisible rope held them together. It was only when they were making their way up through the next summit that the rope seemed to break momentarily.

For suddenly, there was another vehicle on the road. It was the first one Casey had come across since turning onto the highway. There had been one behind Bruen here and there, but none that could be considered possible danger. Until now.

Casey definitely considered the old camper now in front of her a real danger, for it was making its way slowly up the twisting mountainside, slowing her considerably. There was nothing to do but squeeze past it, for Bruen was now gaining.

Casey took her chance the moment she saw it. She was past the camper. With any luck she could put enough miles between them, to lose Bruen in Stanley. She took a deep breath and concentrated on her driving. One mile...two. She was over the summit, racing down the other side. Mile ate up mile. She was going as fast as she dared in the darkness. The road twisted and turned, then seemed to straighten itself out. She was in Stanley, and, she needed gas.

She turned into the city weaving down several empty streets. There wasn't a service station open. She dared not go back to the highway. Instead, she turned toward the old mountain roadway she had to take, hoping against hope she would find a service station there. She did, but it too, was closed.

Casey climbed out in frustration, trying the pumps. They were all locked. No! They weren't all locked. The pump containing premium was not. The lock was there, but it hadn't been shut.

Casey removed the lock, and began filling her tank, unable to believe her good fortune. Or was it good fortune?

Intuition made her glance up the road. A car was bearing down on her; a car with a single yellow parking light.

No! She flung the hose away from her and dove back into her car and shot out of the service station onto the old road. Bruen's car was now only a minute or two behind hers.

No! She cried silently. It wasn't possible! She had lost him. It wasn't possible that he could find her again! But he had.

Casey didn't bother glancing back. She pushed down on the pedal, turning her whole concentration back to her driving as she skidded around a curve. The road was nothing more than a two lane road; a narrow, two lane road that snaked in and around the mountains as it rose and fell. Though it looked as if it had been paved recently, its curves were not banked and only half of them had guard rails of any sort.

Still, she pushed it, speeding around every twist and turn. She had to. She was too tired to think of any other way out. She had lost them twice and twice they had found her again. How? How could they hone in on her every time? How could they?

Casey's heart lurched. *They were honing in on her!*

But how?

A transmitter! She groaned, hitting the steering wheel in both frustration and anger. How could she have assumed that it was a bullet they had shot at her? That hole had been twice the size necessary! Why, oh, why, hadn't she checked her trunk!

"Okay," she muttered aloud, taking a firmer grip of the steering wheel. It did no good to lose them. She had to outrun them. She had to get to Raccoon Creek before them. Then she could let Keir and his father take care of the homing device; take care of them. The fact that Keir and his father were in all probability miles away in Washington no longer entered her head. Keir was there waiting for her, Keir, as well as Cortney and Chenin and his parents.

A slight smile played on her lips as she thought of them all, thought of the joy she would see in Chenin's face...of the surprise in Dajon Jairon's as she opened the medallion.

Her thoughts were cut short as a car suddenly loomed in front of her. She slammed on her brakes and skidded, coming to a stop barely six inches from the edge of the road.

She sat where she was a moment, shaking. The car in front of her rambled on around the mountain.

The car behind her was gaining.

Casey shot her mustang back on the road and caught up with the rambling car. She tooted her horn and flashed her bright lights on and off.

"Come on!" she cried, but it was to open air. The driver continued to ramble on at the same slow speed.

Bruen was still gaining.

"Oh, God," Casey whispered as she pulled into the opposite lane. "Oh, God. Help...help me." She pulled around the car and went around the curve of the road before pulling back into her lane.

She couldn't take much more. She wiped the tears from her eyes with a shaky hand. She was exhausted. She had to stop. She had to lose Bruen because she wasn't going to make it.

Yet she drove on.

She passed another car, this one abandoned half over the edge of the cliff, looking as though it had been there awhile. She shook her head then caught her breath as the idea hit her. There was only one way to be rid of Bruen and that was to give him what he wanted; an end to the chase.

But it would not be the kind of end he would expect.

She glanced in her rear view mirror then stepped slowly down on the accelerator. She would need time; three, maybe four minutes. And she had to find the right place.

Both came to her twenty minutes later. The curve was perfect; a sharp left turn at the bottom of a rather straight downhill stretch. There was no guard rail. Bruen would be able to see the car go over, but hopefully, not her.

Twenty feet from the curve, Casey jammed on her brakes and eased her mustang closer to the edge of steep drop just off the road. She jumped from the car, and with a furtive glance at the top of the hill, she raced to the edge making sure there was nothing that would stop her car from going over.

Nothing but a few branches that she kicked out of the way. She moved quickly back to her car. She had to make sure her car was as close as she could get it to the edge of the drop. She would have little time to push. It took her longer than she had expected. She set her car in neutral and closed its door. She barely had time to round the car before Bruen's car came into sight at the top of the rise. Casey turned and pushed.

Her mustang didn't budge. She desperately pushed again, giving it all her strength. She felt it rock and heaved against it even harder, pushing until she felt her muscles would snap under the strain.

Her mustang however, began moving slowly forward. One inch…two…a foot. Then suddenly it was falling over the edge. Casey's hand caught on the bumper and for an awful moment she thought she would go over with the car. Her hand pulled free.

With her heart in her throat, Casey turned and raced around the curve, praying that the headlights from Bruen's car hadn't caught her movement. She reached the safety of the trees above the curve and then stopped and looked back.

It was over in a split second.

Bruen's car did not slow. Instead of stopping where her car had gone over, it sailed over the edge as well. Casey heard metal hitting metal, then an explosion closely followed by another.

Without a backward glance, Casey turned and ran.

Chapter TWENTY-TWO

R accoon Creek.

Casey stared at the sign, then at the campground beyond. They were here. She only had to find Keir's van…

There was no van. The dirt road rambled around campsites, keyed, and went back as it had come, and there was no van. She had been wrong.

Casey stood helplessly in the dirt road. She felt dead… tired, hopeless, and empty…and dead. And then, out of nowhere, she heard them.

"Casey? *T'Casey!*"

Cortney stood at the edge of the road staring at her as she stood staring at him. The fishing pole dropped from his hand and the next moment she had him in her arms; and then Chenin as well.

"Oh, Casey!" Cortney cried. "I was so afraid for you!"

Casey held the trembling little bodies closer. "It's all right," she whispered. "It's all right. It's over."

They clung to her tightly; wordlessly, but then words were unnecessary. They were safe, and together, and that was all that mattered.

"Is Keir with you?" Cortney asked, pulling away at last.

Casey slowly shook her head as uneasiness swept through her. "He isn't here?"

"He's on his way," said a quiet voice from behind the child. Casey looked up and found herself gazing at an older edition of Keir. Dajon Jairon. He was taller than his son, and his hair was just beginning to gray, but outside of this the resemblance was marked. His warm eyes met hers briefly then turned to his niece. "Chenin, go tell your aunt that Casey is here. Tell her to fix some tea."

Chenin looked uncertainly at Casey, but did as she was told. By this time Cortney had straightened himself and was once again in control. "Uncle Dajon, this is our T'Casey," he said solemnly, "T'Casey Hammond."

His uncle Dajon took Casey's hands and pulled her gently to her feet. "Miss Hammond."

"Casey."

Dajon smiled. "Casey. It's good to meet you at last. I am Keir's father, Dajon Jairon."

Casey smiled rather unsteadily.

"Come. You are exhausted. You must rest."

But Casey couldn't rest, not while she still held the medallion. She pulled it from her pocket and held it out to Keir's father. "Your brother, I think...he meant this for you."

Dajon looked down at the object she placed in his hand and smiled a sad, faraway smile.

Cortney began to dance. "Casey, you have saved it! You really have saved it!"

"He left what we think is his formula inside it," Casey said quietly. "It contains some sort of a computer chip."

Dajon looked up at her in mild surprise. "So you've found that."

Casey nodded. "It opened when the medallion fell." She took a deep, tired breath. "I was waiting to hear from Keir, but then…they came." She shuddered involuntarily.

Dajon reached out and took her hands again, squeezing them reassuringly. "Hush. Let us worry about them now."

"There's no need," she gulped. "I think…they're dead."

Cortney looked at Casey. "Who's dead?"

"Bruen," his uncle said lightly. "Go pick up the fishing poles, Cortney. We must get Casey back to the cabin."

Casey watched the boy for a moment as he dashed off then turned back to Dajon.

"My car," she said, taking a deep, uneven breath. "You see, I sent it over the embankment. I wanted them to think that…that I was dead. I didn't think…" She stopped and looked up at Keir's father. "They must have thought I was following the road because they…they…"

"Hush, Casey." He drew her to him. "Hush. It's no longer important now. You need to get off your feet, to get some food and some rest. Cortney?"

Casey let herself be led off the road and down a path to the small cabin below. Dajon kept his arm around her, and Cortney walked beside them both.

"Do you like it, Casey?" Cortney was gesturing to the cabin as they drew near. "Chenin and I think it is wonderful!"

It was hard to tell until they rounded the side of the cabin to its front. And then it was impossible. In front of the cabin a new red Jaguar stood gleaming in the sun.

Casey stood staring at it, her heart in her throat. Her cousin's?

It couldn't be! It couldn't...but it was, for he stood standing on the small porch.

"Donald?"

With a small cry she ran up the porch steps and into his arms. They clamped around her like a vice. "Oh, God, Casey," he whispered when he could catch his breath. "We couldn't find you. We found your car...we found *them*...but we couldn't find you. We thought...Oh, Casey, we were so frantic about you!"

Casey fought back her tears. "I'm okay. Really, I'm okay."

Donald's worry was evident. "Are you sure, Casey? When Keir and I--"

"Keir?" Casey pulled away.

Her cousin grinned slowly and turned her toward the open doorway. Casey found herself staring into Keir's white face.

"Casey?"

His voice cracked and he reached out and pulled her into his arms. They clamped painfully around her. "Oh, Casey." His body shuddered and he crushed her tighter against him. "Thank God...Oh, thank the Mighty God!"

Casey closed her eyes, letting the tears that she had held at bay for so long cascade quietly down her cheeks. She was safe. At long last she was safe...and in Keir's arms where she belonged.

"Keir." His father's voice was quiet.

Keir's head slowly came up.

"You best sit down with her before you both fall down. She's exhausted."

Keir nodded, but wouldn't let her go and Casey found herself on the sofa, still encased in his arms. Donald planted himself down beside them.

"Better?"

She nodded and he reached over and squeezed her arm. "I don't ever want to go through another night like that one."

"Neither do I," she heard Keir shudder. His arms tightened. She felt his lips on her head and her eyes closed. She nestled into the security of his embrace with a deep sigh of relief…

Though Dajon went and called the authorities to report the accident they didn't arrive until much later. Casey had to be roused from Keir's lap to talk to them. Too tired to worry about it, she told the story Dajon had told her to tell. She had simply pulled off the road there at the turn to walk around and get a breath of fresh air before she went on. The next thing she knew, the car coming down the road had rammed into hers and both cars had gone over the cliff. Donald and Keir had told how they had come across the burning mess shortly after, had looked for survivors, and had then driven on to the campground to report it, finding and picking Casey up along the way. All three denied having any knowledge of the men in the black car.

The two officials accepted what they had said, took notes and left, leaving them in peace. Casey curled herself back into Keir and closed her eyes. She was asleep almost instantly.

Chapter TWENTY-THREE

"Casey?"

"Hmm?" She snuggled down deeper into the covers, not quite willing to let go of the blissful oblivion.

"Ca-sey." She heard a familiar, gentle laugh above her. She opened her eyes.

Keir smiled softly. "Hi, sweetheart."

"Hi," she managed self-consciously, flushing when she yawned.

He bent and planted a soft kiss on her lips. "It's time you were up, *sher'avi.*"

"What time is it?"

"About eight a.m." he said. "You slept through most of yesterday."

"I did?"

"You did."

"Oh."

Keir smiled. "I love you."

Warmth filled Casey. "I sort of suspected that," she smiled up at him. "You gave me your life-ring."

Keir reached down and touched the two small rings lying side-by-side around her neck. "You don't know how I agonized about how you would accept it," he whispered.

Casey looked up at him in surprise. "You agonized over it?"

"Oh, yes."

She bit her lip. "I was so afraid that you had given it to me as a gift of gratitude," she said.

"And yet, even with such doubts, you placed yours beside it." He smiled at her, a smile full of warmth and hope and promises.

A rosy flush tinted her cheeks. "I love you, Keir."

He smiled warmly. "I sort of suspected that." The warm smile faded and he sat down on the bed. He took her hand in his. "Casey, you left." The statement held question.

"I'm sorry," she whispered.

"Oh, Casey." He kissed the palm of her hand. "When you told me you were leaving…" He stopped and shook his head.

"I'm sorry." Her eyes met his. "I thought you were in love with someone else."

"Only you, Casey."

Casey swallowed, still unsure. It didn't explain…"I overheard you talking to your mother on the phone. You told her that you hadn't been leading me on, that I've known from the beginning that you were getting married."

He sent her a look of confusion that slowly dawned into one of understanding. "Casey, it wasn't about you, not directly. I was talking to my mother about Chenin. She was worried that Chenin had begun to think that she and Cortney might be allowed to live with me. It was you, *sher'avi,* I was talking of marrying."

"Oh."

He smiled gently and stole a kiss. "Do you know what *sher'avi* means?" he asked softly.

Casey shook her head, unable to withdraw her eyes from his.

"It means my heart's love. You, Casey, are my heart's love. You have been right from the beginning."

"From the beginning?" The warmth inside her expanded.

"From the beginning." He smiled warmly. "You had my attention from the first moment Karl sent me chasing after you," he went on, his hand tightening around hers. "You amazed me, Casey, with your bravery, with your intelligence and your warmth and compassion for two scared children. You had such spirit, even captured."

"I fought you."

A warm grin came out of him. "Yes, and then to protect you, I kissed you. You've been my heart's love since."

"There was no one else?" She had to be sure.

"Only you, Casey. When you asked me to describe my future wife, it was you I described."

"Oh."

"Oh?" A beloved eyebrow rose.

She smiled up at him. "So when do I get to marry you?"
"Just as soon as it can possibly be arranged," he growled.

"Oh, Keir," she whispered, liking the sound of that.

His mother was suddenly standing in the open doorway. "Keir."

"Yes, mother?" His warm eyes had remained on Casey.

"I suggest you get out of there and let her get dressed. Breakfast is just about ready."

He smiled ruefully at Casey. "Mom left some clothes for you over on the chair. I best leave and let you get into them." He bent and planted a soft, lingering kiss on her lips. "Don't take too long," he whispered.

"I won't. I love you, Keir."

"Get dressed, *avi*." He bent and kissed her again before disappearing out the door.

She called him back.

He swung his head around the doorway. "What is it, Casey?"

"Close the door?"

He grinned, then kissed the tip of his fingers and saluted her with them before pulling the door gently shut. Casey giggled. She would never tire of that man. He may drive her crazy half the time, but she definitely would never tire of him!

She crawled out of bed with a laugh and hurriedly dressed in the cut-off jeans and T-shirt that had been provided then slipped out of the room into the bathroom. She found a comb and ran it through her hair and then brushed her teeth with one of the packaged toothbrushes that had been lying on the counter.

Her cousin grinned at her when she finally emerged into the kitchen. "About time you crawled out of bed!"

Casey stuck her tongue out at him then turned to Chenin who had run up and hugged her.

"You get to sit by me!" said the girl.

Casey grinned at the child. "I get to sit by you?"

"Right here." Chenin pulled out a kitchen chair for her then slipped into the chair beside it. Casey sat down to find Cortney sliding into the chair on her other side. Keir sat across from her and Donald beside him.

"You sleep well?" Dajon asked from the head of the table.

Casey smiled. "Very well. Thank you."

He smiled and held out his hands for grace. "We have much to be thankful for today." His prayer was one of thanksgiving, as well as a blessing, and Casey found Keir's eyes bright on her when he had finished.

I love you, he mouthed.

Her heart jumped. She caught her cousin watching her and felt a slow flush rise in her cheeks.

Donald grinned then raised an eyebrow at her as he took the plate of food Dajon held out to him. "So, when do we hear wedding bells?"

Keir looked up as he took his own plate of food. "As soon as possible. I've chased her long enough!"

His mother looked affronted. "Keir Jairon! That's not a polite way of putting things, nor is it a decision you have the right to decide." She winked mischievously at Casey. "The wedding is up to her, not you."

"Casey, you are going to marry Keir?" Chenin cried excitedly.

Casey flushed and nodded.

"Yes!" both Chenin and Cortney shouted, showering her with hugs.

Donald shook his head. "You poor man," he said to Keir, patting him on the back. "You have no idea what you're getting into. Casey can be so…"

"Donald Walter Hammond. Shut up!"

"Hey, just offering him some sympathy."

"Right." She glanced at Keir. "Did you *have* to bring him with you?"

"Hey, he brought me," Keir protested.

"Oh. Well, in that case, I guess I'll just have to forgive him." She sobered almost instantly. "How did the two of you..?"

"Keir arrived at your apartment just as those goons took off after you," Donald said lightly. "We came together."

"Oh?"

"Keir was trying to reach you before the nadarb could," Dajon said quietly. "Bruen knew you had the medallion."

"We were worried for you, Casey," Cortney said. "They were so terribly mad when they left me."

"They took Cortney and shook him!" Chenin cried. "They shook him hard!"

Casey's eyes flew to Dajon's. He nodded. "They caught Cortney playing in front of Keir's home and demanded the medallion from him. They got a bit rough."

"They hurt him!" Chenin cried again.

Cortney shifted uneasily. "Chenin told them you had the medallion...They left to go after you. They did not hurt you, Casey? Keir promised he would not let them hurt you." His eyes were on her wrist. It had begun to discolor where the car had caught it.

Casey did her best to reassure the boy. "It's all right. It's just a bruise. I hit it on the car." Her eyes went to Keir.

"I tried, Casey. I tried to get to you before they did, but I was too late." His voice was tortured. "You had already fled with them chasing after you yet again."

"We're terribly sorry you were put through that, Casey," Dajon said. "I began phoning the moment Keir went for you, to warn you, but I couldn't get through."

Donald looked up. "Because that blasted phone of hers has been out of commission for a while now."

Casey shook her head in confusion. "How were they able to find Cortney?"

Keir's mother smiled gently. "Your cousin told Keir you were still waiting for a letter from him. We think now they intercepted it for the address."

Casey's eyes turned to Keir. "You wrote?"

"I wrote."

"Oh." Her lips curved into a smile. "What did you say in your letter?"

Keir froze as the table had stilled. A hint of a flush ran up his neck. "That is for your ears alone, *avi*."

Donald laughed.

"Here's coffee," Keir's mother said, setting down the coffee pot and a tray of mugs. "Why don't you go out on to the porch and drink it, while I clean up in here?"

"Good idea." Keir's father picked up a mug and with a kiss to his wife led the way outside. The rest of them followed suit. Casey was surprised to find Donald's arm around her.

"I like your Keir," he whispered to her. "I like him a lot."

She dimpled. "I'm glad you approve. I like him a lot, too."

Donald laughed. "Well, I should hope so."

She looked up and smiled as Keir joined them.

"You're coffee okay?"

"Wonderful."

He kissed her on the tip of her nose, then casting a quick glance at his father, kissed her slowly, though briefly, on the lips. He flushed as he caught Donald's eyes on him.

"Maybe the two of you should take a quiet, morning walk," Donald said solemnly. His eyes danced.

Keir laughed softly, his eyes flickering to Casey. "Maybe we should." Without waiting for her acceptance, he took the coffee mug from her hand and handed it to Donald. "I owe you."

He pulled Casey from the porch and down a small, well-worn path. A minute later, he turned down a smaller path.

Casey looked up at him. "Where are we going?"

"On a quiet, morning walk, just as your cousin suggested."

Casey smiled. "He likes you."

"And I like him." He led her into a secluded, grassy area surrounded by trees and bushes then stopped and pulled her into his arms. "But I love you," he breathed, his lips immediately descending to hers. "I love you, Casey." And then he was kissing her, thoroughly… deeply… longingly. Lovingly.

A deep groan escaped him as he cradled her against him. "Oh, my, but I've needed that, Casey. I've needed you. I've missed you so much."

"And I've missed you...terribly." She looked up at him, begging him silently to kiss her again.

He complied, sending warmth all the way to her toes. "Oh, my."

He nuzzled a kiss into her neck. "You won't make us wait to be married, will you, Casey?"

"No."

She was kissed thoroughly for her answer.

Casey contentedly melted against him. "But I would like a church wedding," she said.

"Yes...Not a big wedding, I hope?"

"No. Just family would be fine...maybe a few friends. Would that be all right?"

"Oh Casey." He cradled her face gently in his hands. His heart was in his eyes; his voice soft. "Believe it or not, I wouldn't want it any other way." He kissed the tip of her nose and smiled down at her. "I can't wait to see you in your wedding dress. To see you walk down that aisle for me alone." He brushed his thumbs gently across her cheeks. "I will be the proudest man alive, Casey, to have you to cherish for the rest of my life."

Tears welled in Casey's eyes. "I love you, Keir."

"As I love you, *sher'avi,*" he returned as his lips came down on hers once again. "Oh, Casey, as I love you."

"Keir?"

"Yes, wife?"

Casey's heart turned. She still hadn't gotten used to being called wife. They had only been married a week. This was their first day back from their honeymoon.

She giggled. She had not made Keir wait long at all. They had married in a small church wedding just a mere six weeks after leaving Raccoon Creek. Family had attended, including Henry and Janet, as well as just a few close friends on both sides. Donald had been the best man and Chenin the flower girl. It had been perfect.

"Breakfast is almost ready," she called up the stairs.

"Coming." But she heard no sounds of him making his way down. Casey went back to the kitchen.

She roamed through the newspaper while she waited for the toast to pop up; while she waited for Keir to come downstairs. This would be their first breakfast together since returning from their honeymoon. She wanted it to be perfect.

She also wanted to find the newspaper page that held the wedding pictures. Their photo should be in it by now.

She scanned the headlines curiously as she turned the pages. And then she saw it; the small obscure article close to the bottom of the page. Her heart started beating wildly.

"*Keir!*"

She heard him clamor down the stairs. "Casey?"

She stared at him as he rushed into the kitchen, her eyes swimming.

"Casey, what is it?"

"Read this," she managed, holding the paper shakily out to him.

Keir took the paper tentatively from her and read the article she pointed out:

Scientist Davin Neal Jairon, after having defected from his Soviet ruled country of Thern, has been granted asylum by the United States government. Jairon made his escape during an explosion that had ripped apart the complex where he and his colleagues worked. Spending months in hiding, Jairon made his way to the United States Embassy in Sweden where he turned himself over to the American government. Jairon intends to reside with family already in the United States.

Casey and Keir stared at one another, a slow grin spreading across their faces. Life was good. So very, very good.

★★★